# Am I Right or Am I Right?

# Am I Right or Am I Right?

## Barry Jonsberg

ALFRED A. KNOPF 🐎 NEW YORK

THIS IS A BORZOI BOOK PUBLISHED BY ALFRED A. KNOPF

Published in the United States by Alfred A. Knopf, an imprint of Random House Children's Books, a division of Random House, Inc., New York. Originally published in Australia by Allen & Unwin under the title *It's Not All About You, Calma.*

www.randomhouse.com/teens

Educators and librarians, for a variety of teaching tools, visit us at www.randomhouse.com/teachers

*Library of Congress Cataloging-in-Publication Data*
Jonsberg, Barry.
Am I right or am I right? / Barry Jonsberg. — 1st American ed.
p. cm.
Originally published under the title, It's not all about you, Calma.
Australia : Allen & Unwin, 2005.
Summary: Sixteen-year-old Calma Harrison is certain she knows what is behind the strange behavior of everyone in her life, and convinced that she is the only one who can fix things, but soon learns just how wrong she is.
ISBN 978-0-375-83637-4 (trade) — ISBN 978-0-375-93637-1 (lib. bdg.)
[1. Interpersonal relations—Fiction. 2. Single parent families—Fiction. 3. Schools—Fiction. 4. Poetry—Fiction.] I. Title.
PZ7.J7426Am 2007
[Fic]—dc22
2006016464

Printed in the United States of America
February 2007
10 9 8 7 6 5 4 3 2 1
First American Edition

*For Nita . . . by far*

# Am I Right or Am I Right?

# Chapter 1

## Six snippets

### One

It was a wet-season day in the tropics. Swollen clouds swept in from the south and squatted over my house. A massive clap of thunder shook the floors and gave the signal for the clouds to discharge their load. A gentle drumroll of rain on the roof built to a thrumming crescendo. The temperature dropped instantly by ten degrees. Through the window I could see water flooding off the roof, a curtain enveloping the house. The roar of rain drowned out all other noises.

No one deserved to be outside in that.

The doorbell rang. It usually had the decibel count of a nuclear warning siren, but I could barely hear it against the background clamor. I put down my book and peered out the front window. Even under the best viewing circumstances you could see only a small portion of anyone standing at the door.

Perhaps a profile of buttocks and, if you were lucky, the back of a head. But with the rain the way it was, I couldn't see anything.

I hesitated. Mum was at work and I was home alone. Not normally a problem, but the weather made me wary. Who would be out in such a downpour? To my mind, there were only two possibilities—a mad axe murderer or a religious fundamentalist. If I was really unlucky, it would be the latter. I suppose I could have pretended not to exist, but I'm a person with a social conscience. The weather *was* foul. I'd have let in a cane toad for shelter and a mug of cocoa.

So I opened the door.

The man was below medium height. Actually, well below medium height. He was wearing a white shirt and a broad silk tie decorated with Santa Clauses. He held a dripping bag in one hand and swept sodden, thinning hair from his eyes with the other. Niagara Falls flowed over him. His clothes stuck to his body and as he shifted position I heard the squelch of rainwater in shoes. He looked at me and blinked rain. A small smile, hesitant, unsure, played around his lips.

"Hello, Calma," he said.

"Dad!" I yelled. "My God! Dad! Don't stand out there in the pouring rain, Dad."

His smile broadened.

"No," I added. "Piss off!"

And I slammed the door in his face.

## Two

My local grocery store glories in the name of Crazi-Cheep. It's one of those places that advertises on local TV channels by assembling a cast of plug-ugly employees dressed in spectacularly nasty uniforms and forcing them to sing a song with banal lyrics, written by a tone-deaf lower primate. The employees all look embarrassed, and so they should. You could force slivers of red-hot bamboo up my fingernails and lash me with rusty barbed wire and I still wouldn't do it.

The employees are very young, presumably so the company can pay them about two dollars an hour and pass on the savings to customers. Crazi-Cheep closes the checkouts by degrees during peak times, so ultimately there is a line of fifty people at one register, staffed by a pubescent operator prone to pimples, lank hair, and narcolepsy. You can visibly age in one of their lines. Not that anyone would notice, because most of the customers are so old they'd be candidates for carbon dating.

Crazi-Cheep is not high on my list of not-to-be-missed shopping experiences.

This, however, was an emergency. I braved the depressing canned music—a compilation CD probably entitled *Major Manure of the Seventies*—and took my place in a line whose length might have been justifiable if they were handing out free hip replacements. The old lady in front of me was certainly a worry. It was only the fact that she wheezed from time to time that indicated she was still breathing.

Time passed. I grew a few centimeters and the old lady

shrank a few. The CD was on repeat and a particularly annoying track came on again. Finally it was almost my turn to be served.

In Sicily they call it the thunderbolt. I read about it somewhere. It's when you see someone and all these hormonal reactions kick in. Your heart thumps, you sweat profusely, your stomach dips to your shoelaces, and bits and pieces you didn't know you possessed start tingling like you've been plugged into an electric socket. Well, that's what happened to me when I saw . . . him.

I don't want you to think I am a shallow, superficial person, so I won't start with his physical appearance.

Stuff it. Of course I will.

He was tall and rangy. As I watched him scan a tin of Spam (and he did it so effortlessly, with such grace and ease of movement, like a balletic sequence), I caught the hint of lean muscles flexing beneath the uniform. I could picture him on a beach, the sun reflecting off defined biceps and pectorals you could graze your knuckles on. His face was classically sculpted, high cheekbones framing a pert and flawless nose. His eyes were deep brown, liquid with sensitivity and hidden passion; his olive skin gleamed beneath the overhead fluorescent lights. During a particularly tricky scanning maneuver, involving shrink-wrapped bok choy, he parted his full lips to reveal faultless, even teeth. Glossy black hair fell in a perfect curtain over his left eye.

Basically, he was all right, if you like that kind of thing.

As for his personality (*the* most important factor, of course), well . . . hey, how the hell would I know? I stood there with a glazed expression on my face, like someone had smacked me around the head with a frozen chicken carcass. Luckily the old dear in front of me was not the most efficient of customers. The Greek god had finished scanning her groceries and she was gazing into the middle distance with rheumy eyes.

"That'll be twenty-five dollars and fifty-five cents, please," he said.

I loved him for the "please." What a polite and considerate young man! And his voice was like honey dripping over truffles . . .

"Hey?" said the crone.

"Twenty-five dollars and fifty-five cents, please."

She looked amazed, like the last thing she had been expecting was to have to pay for the groceries. I knew what would come next. She'd burrow into her bag for her wallet, which would be right at the bottom. She'd pull out bus passes, framed photographs of her grandchildren, a prosthetic leg, and a packet of surgical bandages and each item would be placed carefully on the counter. Finally, when she had accumulated enough material to fill a Dumpster, she'd find the wallet, count out the sum in nickels, and painfully repack. Then she'd want her FlyBuys card, which would be in a secret compartment at the bottom of her handbag, and we'd go through the whole process again.

This time, though, I wasn't complaining. It gave me the chance to drink in every detail of Jason's appearance. Jason. He had a little name tag. I love the name Jason. Don't you love the name Jason? It's classical and conjures images of flashing swords, short tunics, and Golden Fleece. I was so struck I didn't have time to panic. It hadn't occurred to me that once the old lady had hobbled off it would be my turn to be served and, for a moment at least, Jason's attention would be focused on me.

When he turned to me, my hair clogged up with grease and four pimples spontaneously erupted on my nose. I wanted to die.

And then it got worse. I remembered what I had been standing in line for half a millennium to purchase. It was clamped in my hand. I froze. I wanted to turn back, but forty-five pensioners were behind me and they didn't look friendly. With a sinking feeling, I placed my purchase on the belt and watched it slide towards Jason.

Feminine hygiene products. Or FHP, as I like to call them.

Hang on. Don't get me wrong. I know it's nothing to be ashamed of. The trouble was it was Crazi Brand FHP. I mean, Crazi Brand. Not even FHP in a cool, sophisticated box that hinted at a high-flying businesswoman with a cell phone and investment properties on the Gold Coast. Just a tacky white box with Crazi Brand in big green letters. They should be labeled Cheapskate Crap for Losers. It would be more honest.

Jason smiled at me.

"How are you today?" he said.

It briefly crossed my mind to reply, *Great, thanks, Jason. In full flow and deliriously happy.* I didn't, though. Instead I mumbled, "Good." Can you believe that? *Good!* Boy, I blew him away with wit and sharp repartee there, didn't I?

"That'll be two dollars twenty cents, please."

I dug in my purse for a five. I could feel the pimples on my nose pulsing. They were probably flashing in sequence. If it had been dark, they could have used my face for disco lighting. Forty-five pensioners break-dancing in the aisles.

Look, by that stage, I just wanted to get out. With any luck, Jason might not have noticed me. Not properly. Not enough to recognize me in the future. I tried to keep my lank, greasy hair over my face. Thank God I wasn't wearing a name tag.

"Calma Harrison, is that you?"

The woman behind me tapped me on the shoulder. There was not much I could do. I turned. It was Mrs. Elliott from the library. I had known her since I was four years old—I virtually lived at the library until the age of eleven. She was well past retirement, but no one cared because she was popular with customers, sharp as a razor blade, and knew her books. The way she talked about Charles Dickens, you got the impression they had hung out together at the local mall. Normally I would have been happy to see her. Now, I wanted to shrivel.

"Hi, Mrs. Elliott," I said.

Jason handed me my change and I tried to slink away. Mrs. Elliott was having none of it. She piled the rest of her groceries on the belt and continued to talk.

"My goodness, Calma. Those pimples look angry. Are you washing your face properly, dear?"

Not knowing she was one remark away from hospitalization due to an unfortunate accident with my fingers and her eyes, Mrs. Elliott continued blithely.

"Ah," she said, glancing at my purchase through the transparent supermarket bag. The plastic was so thin it could be

7

measured in microns. They have expensive machines in hospital laboratories that can't cut as thin. "I understand. I always used to get a bad complexion at that time of the month myself."

I was surprised she could remember that far back. I wasn't surprised things were getting worse and worse. An involuntary fart would have capped the whole experience.

"They're for my mother," I said.

*Calma, you are a sad, depressing individual.*

"Look, Mrs. Elliott, I've got to fly," I continued, backing away. "See you soon."

"Get some ointment for those pimples, dear," she yelled at me as I scuttled through the automatic door. "And resist the urge to squeeze them."

I headed for home. Our attic was a small crawl space and I was staying in it until I was forty.

## Three

I'm learning heaps in English. Year 11 sure is a step up in complexity.

My class learned about unreliable narrators today.

Okay. Pin back your ears and pay attention. I'm only going to tell you once and there will be a test at the end. Ready?

I am a narrator and I am unreliable.

All narrators are unreliable, because all people are unreliable. We might not lie, exactly, but our narration is colored by our experiences, our prejudices, or our misconceptions. One person's truth is not another person's truth.

With me so far? Good.

Readers of a novel written in the first person, therefore, shouldn't necessarily believe the "I" within the narrative is telling the objective truth. Because the objective truth doesn't exist. Try as the narrator might, he or she is bound to be unreliable because human frailties afflict us all.

Good stuff, eh?

So. Where does all of this leave us: *you*, the reader, and *me*, the narrator? Let me tell you. Unless I am much mistaken, you want to know about my father. You are probably curious about why I was so hostile toward him. Something has happened in the past, you are thinking. Well, take a prize off the top shelf. And guess who is going to tell you the nasty, sordid details? Me, obviously. I'm the narrator. But as a narrator, I'm unreliable, so how do you know if what I'm saying is accurate? It's a problem. So here's what I'm going to do. I am going to try, really hard, to be as objective as I can. I'll let you know the facts in plain words, like a newspaper article. I will avoid:

1. Any display of emotion
2. Any use of colorful language
3. Reference to any event that is not historically (*her*storically) accurate
4. Any obvious subjectivity or personality in my writing style

Here goes.

My father—that sleazy, two-timing, pathetic bag of shit—dumped my mother and me when I was in Year 6. Having the sensitivity of a hemorrhoid, and being of an age when his shriveled excuse for an ego was at its most vulnerable, he spent his evenings drooling over the cleavage of a twenty-year-old barmaid in the local pub. This woman, and I use the word in its loosest possible sense, already suffered from repetitive strain injury through the frequency with which she removed her underwear. My father, led by his groin (marginally larger than his brain), suggested they destroy the lives of two innocent people by running off to Sydney together, where she could paint her nails and indulge a passion for skimpy Lycra outfits and he could comb his hair to hide his bald patch. Five years passed before my father, unable to survive without inflicting pain and misery on another human being, returned to the tropics and attempted to make contact with those he had abandoned. This vile slug had not contacted us in five years, and now he oozed back in search of forgiveness, hot meals, and air-conditioning—not necessarily in that order.

Okay. Those are the facts. Now you can form your own judgment.

Four

I had a poem to write for English.

Most kids have to write poems for English, nearly all hate it, and even more are crap at doing it. But it is so easy.

So, do you want the Calma Harrison foolproof guide to writing poetry on any conceivable subject in fewer than two minutes? It will change your life. Never again will you dread that assignment. I guarantee you'll pass, and if my experience is anything to go by, you'll probably get an A. No skill or brain-work required. In fact, skill and brains are a disadvantage.

Okay, here goes.

Let's get rid of some misconceptions. Misconception number one: poetry has to rhyme. Wrong. Rhyming poetry is actually very old-fashioned (as well as a pain in the arse to write) and we are modern, up-to-date wordsmiths here. Misconception number two: rhythm is important. Wrong, wrong. Modern poetry relies upon the rhythm of the street, the natural cadences of the spoken language (memorize that and repeat it to any teacher who challenges you). Misconception number three: poetry has to make sense. Wrong, wrong, wrong. Let's be honest. How many proper poems have you read where you've known what the hell was going on? Few, if any, I'll bet. And the same applies to your teacher. He or she will read your poem and nod wisely. They can't admit they don't understand it. They're English teachers, after all. In the unlikely event they ask you to explain, recite the following: "It was my attempt to rationalize the dichotomy between personal emotions and the pressures of modern-day living." That'll shut them up.

Okay. We don't need rhyme, rhythm, or meaning. The key is that it should *look* like a poem.

Let me give you an example. Take any old drivel you can think up in twenty seconds:

*The wind leaned sideways in the town and the boy threw up as I felt excitement pouring down the rain-swept streets.*

Gibberish? You got it! Now watch as I turn it into a master-piece of poetic inspiration:

> the wind
>    leaned
>       s
>       i
>       d
>       e
>    ways in the town
>       and the boy threw
>       p
>    u
>    as i felt excitement pouring down the rain-
>    swept streets

See? It's still crap, but no one knows it's crap. Mucking around with spacing, the shape of lines, and punctuation has made it poetry in motion.

Too bloody easy.

Calma, you're a legend.

Five

*Dear Fridge,*

I don't know how to break this gently . . .

You might remember that twenty years ago, when you were young, inexperienced, and suffering from the bad taste that characterized the early eighties, you fell under the noxious spell of a serial loser called Robert. Instead of spurning him, as one would a rabid dog, you lost the plot to such an extent that you muttered "I do" in front of appalled witnesses at a registry office. I, personally, am inclined to attribute this to temporary insanity produced by excessive substance abuse (rampant at the time), though I don't insist upon this. It may not have escaped your memory, either, that some four years later there was issue from this union in the shape of yours truly. I still hold out hope that this was the consequence of artificial insemination from an anonymous donor.

Be that as it may, the putrid excrescence known as your ex-husband is back, Fridge. He turned up this morning like a bad smell, though I attempted to waft him away. We need to arrange new identities, false passports, and visas for the Galapagos Islands. Give me the word and I'll withdraw the forty-eight dollars from my savings account.

Sorrowfully, your loving daughter,

*Calma*

*Dear Calma,*

Bob's been back a week. Didn't tell you because I knew how you'd react. Wasn't expecting he'd turn up at the house. Sorry. Should have told you.

Put the Galapagos trip on hold and don't withdraw your money. I'd hate to create a crisis in the Australian economy.

Love,

*The Fridge*

## Six

"Calma, could you do me a favor?"

Miss Moss was the best English teacher I'd ever had. She was new at my school, replacing Miss Payne, who'd left under a cloud. And with a police escort. I still couldn't understand how Miss Moss had got the job. She was articulate, intelligent, excellent at English, enthusiastic about communicating her skills, and conscientious to a fault. My school wouldn't normally touch someone with such impeccable credentials. We specialized in the aging and incompetent. The interview panel had obviously made a big mistake, but I wasn't complaining.

"Of course, Miss."

Miss Moss carefully opened the large case on her desk. We were minutes into our first lesson of the new week. It was a pleasure to be in class, not just because of the quality teaching but also because I was with fifteen other students who were eager to learn. We sat in respectful silence while Miss Moss removed a large saxophone from the case and walked over to my desk.

"Could you play us a tune, Calma?" she said, thrusting the gleaming instrument under my nose. I laughed.

"Sorry, Miss," I said. "I can't play sax."

"Oh, go on," she said. "Any tune you like. Make something up."

I took the saxophone from her, only because she wasn't giving me an option. It was lovely and slightly warm to the touch. There was a bewildering array of valves and stops, burnished to a golden glow. I could imagine it had a beautiful tone. But that was academic. I had more chance getting a tune out of a toaster.

"I can't play, Miss."

"Please. Just a short melody."

Now, I liked Miss Moss, but the part of my brain responsible for intellectual irritation was receiving serious stimulation. I mean, I couldn't have been much clearer. It was time for plain speaking.

"Miss," I said. "You don't understand. I can't play saxophone. It's not a question of not wanting to. I can't—meaning I do not have the skill, the ability, the expertise, the know-how, the technique, the requisite musical knowledge, the capacity, the facility, the knack, the gift, or the talent. I can't get a tune out of a jukebox, let alone this." I smiled sweetly. "I hope I've made myself clear."

Miss Moss had returned to her desk and was searching through a drawer. She pulled something out, looked at me a moment, and then held up a sheet of paper.

"So how do you explain this, Calma? Your 'poem.' " I swear I could hear the quotation marks in her voice. "What a sad, pathetic thing you must think the English language is if you can pretend that what you have written here is anything other than cacophonous drivel. I asked you to make music out of words. You didn't. And you are quite right about the saxophone. No one would expect someone without talent to make music from it. But you are talented at English, Calma. You *can* make words sing. You have the capacity, the skill, the gift, and the talent. Which makes *this*"—she waved the sheet again, as if

**15**

trying to shake it to death—"all the more deplorable. If you want to desecrate your abilities, then fine. It's your choice. But don't expect me to be pleased or to collude with you in it. ' 'Sblood. Do you think I am easier to play on than a pipe?' "

I could feel my face flush. I fixed my eyes on the desk.

"Trivia question, class. From which play did that quote come? Answers to me at the beginning of next lesson. First correct to receive a completely pathetic prize."

The class laughed.

"Right. Last week we considered the unreliable narrator. Let us continue. Please turn to the first page of Jane Austen's *Emma. . . .*"

I cradled the saxophone on my knees for the rest of the lesson. When the bell rang I waited until everyone had gone, then placed it back in its case. Miss Moss was wiping the whiteboard.

"That was unfair," I said. "Why did you humiliate me?"

Miss Moss turned.

"You humiliated yourself, Calma," she said. "I was teaching you."

We stared at each other for a while. Tears pricked my eyes. My next class was a free period and I needed to think. I was nearly out the door when Miss Moss called my name.

"The quote, Calma?" she said.

"Hamlet," I said, "to Rosencrantz and Guildenstern."

Miss Moss waited until I forced myself to meet her eyes. She smiled.

# Chapter 2

## Getting to know your narrator

Hi! Here at *Hot Gossip* we pride ourselves on keeping you up-to-date with your fave celebs. Who's in, who's out, who's halfway in, who was in but has just popped out for five minutes, who's out but thinks they're in, and who's inside out and upside down. This week we have an exclusive interview with the hottest property in town, our own homegrown Aussie chick who's taking Tinseltown by storm: Calma Harrison.

HG: *Hi, Calma. Thanks for taking time out of your busy schedule to talk to us.*

CH: *Always a pleasure.*

HG: *Your career is the stuff of legend, Calma. How have you managed to achieve so much at just sixteen years of age?*

CH: *Well, clean living plays a part. I exercise regularly, eat good, nutritious food, and always get eight hours of sleep a night. But mostly it's because I am enormously talented.*

HG: *Yes, indeed you are. And* Time *magazine recently*

named you the most beautiful woman in the world. Would you care to comment?

CH: *Well, it's silly, isn't it? I mean, look at me. I'm five foot nine, 135 pounds. I have brown eyes, a flawless complexion, silky chestnut hair, and a bust that on occasions is in a different time zone than the rest of me. It's absurd to say I am the most beautiful woman in the world. There must be at least two who are more beautiful.*

HG: *I don't think so.*

CH: *No, I don't think so either.*

HG: *What about your upbringing, your home life? Can you tell us about the real Calma Harrison?*

CH: *I live in northern Australia. In fact, I attend a high school there and am currently in Year 11. English is my favorite subject.*

HG: *Which brings us neatly to your latest novel. Is there any truth in the rumor you are a shoo-in for the Nobel prize for literature this year?*

CH: *I can't possibly comment. Let's just say I have a plane ticket for Stockholm, I love pickled herring, and my ski gear is packed.*

HG: *As the reigning Winter Olympics champion in the grand slalom, you must be looking forward to getting on the piste again. But back to your home life. Is it true your father deserted you when you were in Year 6?*

CH: *That is true. But there is always something positive to take from life's little tragedies.*

HG: *You are referring to your latest album,* I Turned Over a

Stone and My Father Crawled Out, *which recently went platinum in the U.S.?*

CH: *Yes.*

HG: *Why do you call your mother "the Fridge"?*

CH: *Since my father left, she has worked constantly because she has an irrational fear of claiming benefits to which she is entitled. She prefers to work herself into a stupor to provide for us. As a result, she is rarely at home and we communicate mainly through notes on the fridge, hence my reference to her in those terms. I see more of the fridge than I do of my mother. But all this is very personal and I'd sooner not go into it.*

HG: *Did you draw on this experience for your Academy Award–winning role in* The Fridge and Me, *written by you, directed by Spielberg, and also starring Robert De Niro and Orlando Bloom?*

CH: *Partly.*

HG: *Are you surprised that your habit of wearing large colored glasses has become something of an international fashion statement?*

CH: *I confess I was flattered when the queen started imitating me—though putting them on the corgis was excessive. But yes, it amuses me to see them on the Australian prime minister.*

HG: *Tell us, Calma, what's going on with your love life? Is there a hottie on the scene, and should we read anything into the pouting jealous rages of a certain Hollywood star whenever you are at a function together?*

CH: *The tabloids have blown that out of all proportion. For the record, her husband and I are just good friends. But yes, there* is romance in the air. I can't say anything yet, but the name Jason is one to listen for.

HG: *You heard it in* Hot Gossip *first. Calma, we know you have groundbreaking work to do on a cure for cancer, and you are scheduled to deliver a keynote address to the General Assembly of the United Nations first thing in the morning. Thanks so much for talking to us.*

CH: *My pleasure.*

# Chapter 3

## Pressures on the Fridge

It was time to get a job.

I had come to this decision for a number of good reasons. I was of an age where I *should* be contributing to the family budget, thus taking pressure off the Fridge. Of course, a little extra personal spending money wouldn't go amiss either. While my classmates were showing off their latest cell phones, with still-image manipulators, video capture cards, wireless Internet, and espresso-making facilities, I couldn't afford two baked-bean cans connected by garden twine.

It was a tad embarrassing.

The most compelling reason, however, was that I needed exposure to real life. As a student, I was living in an ivory tower. I went to classes; I came home and read or watched TV. If I was going to be a writer—my chosen career path and current burning ambition—then I needed to connect with ordinary people and understand their motivations, lifestyles, and patterns of speech. I'd read that proper writers carry a notebook in which they record snippets of conversation that might be of use. I liked that idea.

So, a job. No time like the present. I showered and washed my hair twice before styling it for an hour, so it looked natural. I applied cleanser, toner, reinvigorating face mask, de-wrinkler, energizing lotion with beta hydroxy acids plus supplementing minerals and a few other things in bottles I stole from Mum's collection. Then I started on makeup. The pimples on my nose weren't angry anymore; they were beside themselves with rage. So I applied a masking compound, not unlike the stuff you use to seal shower doors, but skin-toned. It wasn't bad, either. When I'd finished, you couldn't really see the pimples, though there were still bumps, like molehills, along my nose. Short of taking an orbital sander to them, there wasn't much more I could do. I tried to finish the rest of my makeup, but frankly it's an art form I've yet to master. After much screwing up of the eyes and facial contortions, I managed to end up looking relatively normal—a considerable improvement on my usual efforts, where I wouldn't be out of place in a Picasso painting. I turned to the wardrobe.

Something elegant yet businesslike. Something that would say "serious job seeker" yet at the same time reflect my personality. Two hours later I had tried every possible combination of shirts, blouses, skirts, pants, T-shirts, tops, dresses, and sundry clothing items that did not fit readily into any category. It was like a small detonation had occurred in my wardrobe, scattering everything over the entire bedroom. Finally I settled on a crisp white blouse and a stylish knee-length blue skirt. Next, shoes . . .

A mere five hours after I had started I was ready to take on the world of employment. Donning green plastic-framed glasses, I stepped into the blazing heat of a wet-season afternoon. Now, where could I find a part-time job?

It struck me with the force of revelation. Why not the local Crazi-Cheep? After all, it was . . . local. And I didn't really have any specific skills. It wasn't as if I was passionately into kittens or frill-necked lizards and felt that a pet store would be the only place worthy of my talents. I could scan stuff. I mean, I had seen the staff at Crazi-Cheep. Just how difficult could it be? And it was . . . local. It was perfect. In fact, I decided it was so perfect I wouldn't consider employment anywhere else. I headed purposefully in its direction.

The customer service desk was attended by a girl fresh out of preschool. She chewed gum and studiously ignored me. This was difficult since my glasses by themselves would have stopped a Boeing 747 in flight. Plus I was the only customer. Though I did note, out of the corner of my eye, a lone checkout operator and forty pensioners stretching into the feminine hygiene and car accessory aisle. I stood, a patient smile on my face, while the customer service clerk continued chewing and gazing blankly into the middle distance.

"Excuse me," I said finally.

Her eyes slowly came into focus and she turned her head toward me. There were things in the morgue with quicker reaction times.

"Can I help you?" she asked.

"Not really," I replied. "I just wanted to check if you were some peculiar, life-sized logo, or one of those human statues you see at the markets, or if you were simply in a catatonic state."

Actually, I didn't say that at all. I've gotten into trouble in the past by allowing my mouth off the leash. This time I restrained myself.

"I want to inquire about employment opportunities," I said.

She stared at me, the gum chewing as regular as a metronome. Maybe she was incapable of chewing gum and speaking at the same time. Maybe the number of polysyllables I had used confused her. I watched her tonsils for a while, but, to be honest, they were of limited interest. Finally she pointed to a sign on the counter.

I read it. I was half-expecting something like ABANDON HOPE, ALL YE WHO WAIT HERE. But it said, RECRUITMENT FOR CRAZI-CHEEP STORES IS NOW CONDUCTED BY MISSION IMPOSSIBLE, AUSTRALIA. PLEASE PHONE 555-1011. The girl wore a small smile, as if I was a moron for having missed the notice in the first place. I was encouraged. If she could get employment, then clearly the only criteria for acceptance were basic vital signs and sufficient physical coordination to chew without severing your tongue. I decided to get on it right away.

"Do you mind if I use your phone?" I inquired sweetly.

She reacted as if I'd asked to French-kiss her grandmother.

"It's not for customer use," she said, outrage in her voice.

"I'll pay," I said.

It took a little while to sort it out. This was a scenario she had obviously not encountered before, and having to use her initiative brought on a violent nervous reaction. She lost her gum-chewing rhythm entirely. In the end, though, common sense prevailed and I made an appointment with the recruiting agency for the following afternoon. As I replaced the handset, I was struck by a thought. Why hadn't I considered this before?

"Is Jason working today?" I asked nonchalantly.

"Late shift," she said, her eyes returning to their natural state of vacancy.

Late shift, hey? Just the kind of shift that would suit me perfectly. Life is full of strange coincidences, don't you think? As I went out the automatic doors, I glanced back. The girl was in the same pose, her mouth opening and closing as if she was having a conversation with a goldfish. The line at the open checkout had lengthened. The same CD was droning in the background.

I was going to like this place.

"So what brought this on?" said the Fridge. I had come home and changed into board shorts and a T-shirt. I'd intended to clean up my bedroom but decided I could leave it for a while, accustomed as I was to living in the environmental aftermath of a natural disaster. After another shower to wash off crusty bits of makeup, I went into the kitchen to make a snack and found the Fridge in residence. I was always surprised when I stumbled across her. We were like the trajectories of celestial bodies—once in a long while our paths coincided, and the collision was often spectacular.

"I thought it was a good idea. Help out with the finances, that kind of thing."

The Fridge looked puzzled, as if me helping with money was akin to Osama bin Laden offering to be Santa at the local day-care center. She didn't say anything, though. She sat at the kitchen table and sipped her coffee. I sat opposite. To be honest, I was worried about her. She looked old, her hair splattered with gray. There were frown lines around her mouth that I hadn't noticed before. In fact, her whole face sagged as if a weight was pulling and stretching it. I didn't know what to say. We didn't have a good history of communication.

"Your father dropped in to see me at work today," she threw into the silence. She didn't look at me, and she was chewing the inside of her cheek.

"How charming," I said. "What did you do? Reach for the Raid or call security?"

"He wants to talk."

"What would give him the impression he's got anything to say?"

"He was very serious. Said he needed to talk, that he didn't want anything or to mess up your life."

"Bit late for that, isn't it?" I replied. "Look, be firm and polite and maybe he'll get the message. If that doesn't work, I'll arrange for a couple of muscle-bound acquaintances to visit him with baseball bats."

Mum stared into her coffee cup and continued to chew on her cheek.

"I *will* talk to him, Calma," she said. "And I think you should, too."

I got to my feet. I had a feeling this had been coming. I don't know whom I felt angrier with—my dad for his manipulative power or my mother for allowing him to wield it. However, she was the only available target.

"Are you out of your mind, Mum?" I said. "Have you finally lost it? Do you need reminding what a complete bastard he is? We might not have realized it at the time, but him walking out of our lives was the best thing that could have happened. And now he strolls back in and expects you to listen. He's probably single again, wants to cry on your shoulder about whatever her name was. He treated you like shit. Now, you can't change that. But the very least you can do is make sure he can't treat you like that again. Please don't talk to him, Mum. Please."

"Has it ever occurred to you that your perspective on the past might be faulty, Calma? That not everything is either black or white?"

"I know what I know, Mum. He walked out on us."

"It was all a long time ago, Calma." Her voice was quiet and infused with weariness.

"So what?" I said, my voice getting shriller. "What difference does that make? By that argument, if Adolf Hitler returned, we

would all be going, 'Hey, don't worry. You might have extermi-
nated six million Jews in the gas chambers, but it was all a long
time ago. Have a cup of tea and a Fig Newton.' "

"Your father is not Hitler, Calma. You're overreacting
again."

"No, Mum. You are underreacting. Look what's happened
to us. Here we are having a bloody argument, and over what?
Him. He's been back five minutes and we are fighting. Doesn't
that tell you something?"

"It tells me you like to argue."

I stopped my pacing.

"What? You're saying this is my fault? Oh, I see. Well, it's
pretty obvious when you think about it. Here's me angry and
upset because your low-life ex-husband is trying to worm his
way back into our lives, and it's all my fault. I tell you what,
Mum—you start baking a cake and I'll work on a big banner
we can drape over the front door: WELCOME HOME, SHITHEAD.
FEEL FREE TO FUCK US OVER AGAIN."

I never swear in front of my mother. Her eyes hardened
and her hands clenched into fists. I could see tendons bunch in
her lower arms. Then she relaxed and rubbed her fingers over
her brow, a gesture that seemed to take enormous effort. She
was exhausted.

"I don't want to argue with you," she said in a quiet, reasonable voice that only served to make me angrier. "But you
need to understand that it's not all about you, Calma. When I
make a decision, I take your views into consideration. But the

decision has to be mine. I will not be bullied. By him, by you, by anyone."

She pushed her coffee cup away and picked up the car keys. "I'm off to work."

I had my back to her as she left the house. I didn't trust myself to keep my mouth shut, and saying anything else wasn't going to help. I heard the car start up and the crunch of tires on the gravel as she reversed out. Only when silence settled over the house did I go into the front room and sit down. I tried reading *Emma* for a while but couldn't concentrate.

Mum was right. It wasn't fair of me to use anger to influence her. If my feelings were worked up by the return of my father, then hers must have been in turmoil. The last thing she needed was me churning them up further.

Nonetheless, I couldn't ignore my own emotions. There was trouble ahead. I could only hope we would both be strong enough to deal with it.

# Chapter 4

## Peace offering

*Dear Fridge,*

I'm sorry. I was wrong.

Not as wrong as you, but a lot sorrier.

I want to apologize also for using the word "F***." I know you don't like it. I admit it. I fucked up.

Love,

*Calma*

# Chapter 5

## All about relationships

I got the job!

It was sooo easy. I took along a résumé, filled out a form, and had a short interview with a balding bloke who smelled of tobacco smoke and essence-of-dead-dog cologne.

I nearly choked when he told me the pay rate. I was under the impression child slavery had been abolished. A sudden vision came to me—a muscled manager in a loincloth whipping cowering employees for not keeping up with the rhythm of beating drums. I didn't say anything, though. I even tried to manufacture an expression of unbridled joy at the prospect of working for an hourly sum you'd expect to find down the back of a sofa.

I was due to start on Saturday. Late shift. I'd get a uniform and after three months I would be entitled to a staff discount of 5 percent. Riches beyond my wildest dreams.

I was excited and a little nervous.

*   *   *

English continued to be great. I'd done some serious thinking about Miss Moss. I'm not sure how accurate a picture you might have of my personality yet, but I'll let you in on a secret. I'm not the sort of person to take criticism very well, particularly if it's criticism of my intellect. Miss Moss had been hurtful. But no matter how hard I tried to feed resentment, I couldn't get over the fact that she was right. The poem I had written *was* awful. It occurred to me that I had two options—curl my lip whenever she was around and rag on her to other students, or talk to her about how to improve.

Mature, or what?

She was terrific when I approached her. She gave up a free period to go over the basic principles of poetry writing. And the more she talked, the more excited I got. I wanted to write proper poetry, to express ideas and emotions in powerful and concise language. Miss Moss made it clear this would require work because writing poetry was a frustrating process that involved grappling with words in ways I hadn't yet considered.

The more difficult she made it sound, the more determined I was to succeed. She said she would be delighted to provide constructive comments about anything I wrote.

I tell you, Miss Moss was so good I was terrified she would wake up one morning and wonder what she was doing in a school where students copying out of textbooks was considered state-of-the-art educational practice. It was only a matter of time before she took her skills elsewhere, so I had to take advantage while I could.

It wasn't just Miss Moss who made English enjoyable, though.

You see, I have a new friend.

Now, for most of you, having a friend is probably not an earth-shattering event. You're undoubtedly the sort of person who gets invited to sleep-overs with thirty-eight other people and buys birthday presents at least twice a week. Well, I've always been a loner. I don't make friends easily. Maybe the Fridge is right—perhaps I put people off with sarcasm and what she calls my "love affair with my own intellect." Who knows?

(Roll intro music)

Presenter: *Good evening. This is the six o'clock news and I'm Anton Enus. In breaking news tonight, Calma Harrison has found a friend. Details from our correspondent in northern Australia, Penny Forum. Hello, Penny, are you there?*

Penny: *Good evening, Anton.*

Anton: *What's the latest, Penny?*

Penny: *Well, Anton, as you can see, I'm outside Calma Harrison's house. I must stress we have no official confirmation as yet, but all the indicators are that the rumors sweeping the nation have some basis in fact. Calma Harrison, loner, total loser in the friendship stakes, seems finally to have found someone willing to be her buddy.*

Anton: *Do we know who this mysterious friend might be, Penny?*

Penny: *The name Vanessa Aldrick keeps cropping up, Anton. A girl in Calma's Year 11 English class.*

Anton: *And what do we know about her?*

Penny: *A picture is emerging. Vanessa is tall, willowy, and, according to reliable sources, a genetic throwback to the 1960s. She wears paisley caftans and beads and her hair is long, limp, and features a severe middle parting. I cannot as yet confirm that she also wears a peace symbol around her neck. Indications are she spends most of her time on a different level of existence than the rest of us, making only brief appearances on the planet Earth.*

Anton: *So, in short, a dysfunctional adolescent?*

Penny: *Exactly.*

Anton: *Has Calma made any comment yet? Can we expect a press conference in the near future?*

Penny: *Well, as you can see, Anton, representatives from all the world's major media are camped outside Calma's house. We have CNN, ABC, BBC, Sky, newspaper reporters from the* Age, *the* Australian, *the* Financial Review, *the* New York Times, *the* Washington Post, *the* Guardian, le Monde, *and* Skateboarders Weekly. *As yet, there has been no sign of Calma, but she is definitely inside her home and we expect a statement shortly.*

Anton: *We'll return to that story as soon as there are new developments. Meanwhile, in other news, an intergalactic war craft from a small planet in the constellation Ursa Minor landed today in Sydney, crushing the Opera House and threatening the destruction of the Earth within the next twenty-four hours. . . .*

If I'm going to be strictly accurate, I should say I've got two friends. You see, we signed up for cable.

I have no idea why. I mean, the Fridge never watches television. She just dusts the screen occasionally. But I was excited. We couldn't afford the movie channels, but even so, my viewing options had increased enormously. The first night, I sat down with the remote control and two pounds of popcorn. It was terrific. It was hypnotic. Four hours of surfing later, I knew that instead of four channels of undiluted sewage, I had thirty-five to choose from. There was a documentary on the history of lead miners' wives in the early twentieth century, an American soap opera in which no one could act but everyone's hair was immaculate, a sports channel featuring international synchronized tiddlywinks, and a shopping channel where, apparently, viewers were scrambling for their credit cards to buy ghastly jewelry at inflated prices.

And then, like a gold nugget in a bucket of diarrhea, there was Discovery. Did you know the male seahorse gets fertilized, carries the babies to term, *and* looks after the offspring? The female, I imagine, goes to the pub with her mates to watch football on a plasma screen.

I was hooked.

It would be an exaggeration to say my first evening at work was an unqualified success. But the near-hospitalization of a customer strikes me as an accident that could happen to anyone. Nonetheless, the incident was not one I would have chosen to have witnessed by my supervisor. On the plus side, though, there was Jason. . . .

Okay. I'll just tell you what happened.

I fronted up to Crazi-Cheep at seven-thirty, half an hour before my shift was due to start. The timing was fortunate because I had to get a uniform and suffer a twenty-minute induction on what the job entailed. This was delivered by my supervisor, who, I was dismayed to learn, was none other than the gum-chewing bump on a log who had ignored me on my first visit. Her name was Candy, which struck me as appropriately lightweight. She ran through the basics in a monotone, her eyes never making contact with mine.

Basically, I wasn't going to be operating a checkout until I had proved myself stacking shelves. I got the impression that being on a register was considered the dizzying height of career ambition—not something I could even aspire to until I had three degrees and fourteen years' experience. I tried to look suitably serious, as if being promoted to the checkout was a distant goal, like winning an Oscar for best supporting actress. Not that my expression made any difference—my face was a nonstick surface as far as Candy was concerned.

I was given a checked, sack-like uniform. It hung dispiritedly just below my knees. Then we went to the warehouse area behind the aisles. I must admit I had always wondered what was behind those big plastic curtains, which shows you what a sad life I've led. Without wishing to destroy the romantic dreams of those who've been similarly curious, the answer is: rows and rows of toilet paper, pasta, and jars of stir-fry paste.

My job for the evening was to check stock on the shelves

and replenish any items that were dwindling. I was hoping to get a pricing gun so that I could go around yelling, "Give me all the money from the registers or I'll mark down everything in the store." But it seems they don't use price stickers anymore.

Anyway, I set to with enthusiasm. Before long I discovered the shelves were woefully low on baked beans. I tell you, it was a good job they had employed me. I was right on the case. A woman with a mission. No customer was going to leave Crazi-Cheep with a cold lump of disappointment stemming from a fruitless search for cheddar-flavored baked beans.

I loaded one of those carts that always seem to get in the way when you're a customer and headed for aisle eight. The front left wheel spun at crazy angles and the whole apparatus had an alarming drift to the right. It was all I could do to avoid crashing into grocery displays just asking for annihilation. Finally, though, I lumbered to a stop halfway along aisle eight and started unpacking and stacking cans of baked beans.

I hadn't got very far with this fascinating and skilled activity when there was a bronchitic cough behind me and a shopping cart slammed into my ankles. Has that ever happened to you? Trust me, it is the most painful thing in the world. Carts are designed that way. I imagine a mad scientist somewhere saying to a white-coated colleague, *Right. We have three standard wheels and the fourth is operated by a microchip programmed to randomly choose directions at right angles to the intended trajectory. We have the child seat that traps your fingers. What else? I know—how about positioning the front bumper bar so it causes permanent disability when rammed into ankles?*

I hobbled to my feet, suppressing the temptation to scream a four-letter word beginning with *f* and ending with *uck* at the top of my voice.

A little old lady was beaming at me. She was vertically challenged to the extent that her wrinkled face just peeped over the cart's handle. It was unnerving.

"I'm so sorry, dear," she said.

"I suspect you are not as sorry as I am," I replied. "Might I also suggest that penitence is not generally accompanied by a wide grin?"

"Pardon?" she said.

"What can I do for you?" I asked, rubbing my ankles. The pain had subsided, so it only felt like red-hot darning needles were being inserted into my Achilles tendons.

"Where do you keep your condoms?"

I forgot the pain instantly. Who wouldn't? My jaw dropped, and a range of replies raced through my mind. *On my boyfriend's willie* was the best, but I didn't say it, and not just because I didn't have a boyfriend. With an effort of will, I cranked my lower jaw back up.

"They're for my grandson," she continued. "He wants knobbly ones that glow in the dark."

"Just possibly too much information," I said, "but if you come with me, we'll try to find them."

I *knew* I was going to love this job. I'd only been working half an hour and it was well worth the forty cents I must have earned. If this was going to happen regularly, I'd have paid *them* for the opportunity to work here. Imagine the material I would have for my writer's notebook! If I had one. True, my happiness was dented slightly by the old lady ramming me with the cart again in exactly the same place, but I no longer felt the urge to viciously strike her to the floor.

"I'm so sorry," she said again.

"If you're so sorry," I said, "why do you keep doing it?"

But there was no real anger in my voice. I left her happily poring over the merits of strawberry-flavored Rough Riders and limped back to the baked beans.

I was debating the artistic merits of pyramid displays as opposed to the space-saving yet rather conventional rectangular stack system (who said this job wasn't going to be stimulating?) when another customer behind me coughed and said, "Excuse me?" I tell you, it's an occupational hazard when you're a shelf stacker. People sneak up on you. I got up and turned around.

My father was standing there.

## Fact File

*Common name:* Robert Harrison

*Scientific name: Baldus shortarsius*

*Habitat:* This noxious creature is not, as one might reasonably expect, found under slimy stones, but is liable to appear in any environment when you least expect it. Prefers warm climates but is unable to provide for itself and thus attaches itself to any available host body, where it will cling unpleasantly and eventually empty the refrigerator.

*Mating habits:* Despite its unprepossessing appearance, *Baldus shortarsius* is apparently sexually attractive to deranged members of its own species. It mates and moves on quickly, effectively diluting its own gene pool. This is worrying since the pool was little more than a puddle in the first place.

*Appearance:* Short, stumpy, and follicularly challenged.

*Toxicity:* Close contact is not fatal, though debilitating symptoms might persevere for years. Best avoided unless wearing full body armor.

*Status:* Unfortunately, not extinct.

We eyed each other for what seemed an age. He was trying to smile, but it was more like a smirk. I don't know what my expression looked like, but I suspect *glacial* might approximate. The frozen food section was generating more heat than me.

"Hello, Calma," he said finally.

"What can I do for you, sir?" I said.

His eyes flickered away and he gave a little wave with his hands, a pathetic gesture of helplessness. He tried the smile again.

"Is that all you can say to me?"

"I'm working, sir. If you need help to find products, then I am employed to assist. If not, I must ask that you allow me to return to my task."

He ran a hand through his thin hair, unconsciously smoothing a few errant strands over his bald patch.

"Aw, come on, Calma. Give me a break. I just need a few words. That's all. Is that too much to ask? A few words with my own daughter?" He put his hand on my arm and my flesh shrank from his touch.

"Please remove your hand, sir, or I will be forced to call security."

He let me go and even took a step backward. Out of the corner of my eye, I noticed Candy standing at the end of the aisle, watching.

"Perhaps we could talk when you've finished your shift?" he said. "Please, Calma."

"I don't finish work until five in the morning," I lied. "And then I have to get straight back to my family. Now, if you'll excuse me . . ."

I don't expect you to believe me, but what happened next was a complete accident. I grabbed the rear rail of the cart and swung it around. My intention was to glide effortlessly back into the bowels of the warehouse section. But the front wheel had other ideas. Instead of executing a perfect arc, the cart juddered and slammed into my father's groin. The sharp metal edge of the front rail landed, with sickening accuracy, on the family jewels. A fleeting, disbelieving look passed over my father's face and then he doubled up, emitting a high-pitched scream. I have no idea, obviously, what it is like to have your testicles propelled into your throat, but I can't imagine it's very pleasant. Certainly the writhing, groaning form in front of me didn't appear to be having the time of its life. All color flooded from his face and he groped, in a kind of shutting-the-stable-door-after-the-horse-has-bolted fashion, at his nether regions.

For a moment I felt sorry for him. It quickly passed.

"If you have damaged this cart, sir, you may have to pay compensation," I said.

He didn't say anything—the act of getting air into his lungs was proving difficult enough. Anyway, Candy had suddenly appeared next to us, a look of alarm on her face. She had stopped chewing and I worried that the shock of seeing one of her customers felled like an ox might cause the gum to get stuck in her windpipe. I'm not sure if I could have coped with two people writhing on the ground.

My father eventually stopped behaving like a gaffed fish and brushed aside Candy's expressions of concern. He assured her it was entirely his fault and I was in no way responsible. Finally he limped out of the store, maybe to take up a new career as a soprano. I didn't know, and frankly I didn't care.

Candy was reluctant to accept my explanation of the incident—a deranged customer, with premeditation and malice, hurled his testicles against my cart. But there wasn't much she could do. After all, the customer had accepted responsibility.

I tell you, between the condom-buying granny and the do-it-yourself attempt at circumcision, I was having the time of my life. And things got a whole lot better when I took my break.

I don't know why I went outside. Maybe it was because the Crazi-Cheep staff room was another example of cost-cutting measures. I've seen better-appointed fridges at the local dump. Anyway, a breath of fresh air never goes amiss.

Jason was standing at the corner of the building having a cigarette. Twenty minutes later we'd arranged a date.

Impressed? So you bloody should be. Want to know the secret of my success? Okay. For those of you out there who can't get a guy to eat out of your hand, take the following as an instruction manual.

Jason: Hi! How you doin'?

Calma: Good. How are you? (*Gorgeous, mouth-watering sex-on-a-stick, that's how you are.*)

Jason: Great. I'm Jason, by the way.

Calma: (*I know. Trust me, I know.*) Pleased to meet you, Jason. I'm Calma. (*Don't make any jokes. Please. Don't be the worst of all possible worlds—a sex-on-a-stick dickhead.*)

Jason: This your first evening at work?

Calma: Yes. (*Do you have a girlfriend? If you've got a girlfriend, I'm enrolling in the nearest nunnery first thing in the morning.*) Do I detect an English accent, Jason? (*Or am I losing control of all my faculties in your presence?*)

Jason: Yeah. Guilty as charged.

Calma: Don't worry. We'll let you off, provided you commit no further offenses in the next twelve months. (*Too early to risk a joke?*) Are you in Australia permanently, Jason, or on holiday? (*Because if you want to stay, we could drive into town, get married, and start a family immediately.*)

Jason: My parents moved to Australia twelve months ago, just after I finished my A levels in England. I'm having a year off before I go to university here. I guess that means we're staying.

Calma: Great! (*Why did I say that? Does it smack of over-enthusiasm?*) Do you miss England? (*Do you have a girlfriend you spend all your time writing to?*)

Jason: Football, mainly. What you call soccer.

Calma: Really? I love soccer. (*Never seen it—is that the one with the round ball?*) What team do you support? (*Like I care. Just keep him talking.*)

Jason: Liverpool.

Calma: They're great. Fantastic team. (*Who?*)

Jason: You reckon they've got their tactics sorted?

Calma: Absolutely. ("*Sorted*"! *Whaaat?*) Really talented. Classy players, every one. (*You could be getting in deep crap here, Calma.*)

Jason: Well, not all of them. Obviously, when the team's on song, you won't find a sharper forward line or a more solid midfield anywhere in the Premiership. It's consistency, though. Too many players drifting in and out of games, not backtracking enough when opponents hit us on the break. And that's another thing. We get exposed by pace on the wings. It's all very well having a solid central defense, but if they're drawn by the overlap, you're always going to be stretched out of shape, particularly with a sweeper system, rather than the conventional four-two-four. As for zonal marking—well, it's a load of bollocks. We need to get back to man-to-man.

Calma: I couldn't agree more! (*I couldn't understand less.*)

Jason: We seem to have forgotten Bill Shankly's immortal words: "Football isn't a matter of life and death—it's more important than that."

Calma: Perhaps we could discuss this further on a date? (*Who could forget old Bill . . . oh, shit!*)

Jason: A date?

Calma: Er . . . yeah. Why not? How about Friday? (*Where's*

*a bolt of lightning when you need it? Or a large hole in the ground?)*

    Jason: Friday? Yeah . . . okay.

That's the point at which you exchange phone numbers. Got it? It works every time. I swear.

**From:** Miss Moss <moss.aj@lotis.edu.au>
**To:** Calma Harrison <harrison.c@lotis.edu.au>
**Subject:** Iambic tetrameter

---

Calma,

Let's start with basic rhythm and rhyme. Use iambic tetrameter (four beats to the line, remember) and a straightforward *abba* rhyme scheme. The key is to use enjambment
(run-on lines) to avoid rhythmical monotony. For this first
exercise, I'll let you choose the subject matter.

Have fun!
Miss Moss

## Song for Vanessa

I used to walk in crowds alone
And though I spoke and slept and ate
To mimic life, to ease the weight
Of grief, it failed. I was a phone

That can't connect, a hollow shell.
The world flowed by me while I stood
And watched how others saw the good
That living brings. I stumbled, fell—

But then you caught me, touched my pain
By being there with friendship's kiss.
The truth, I know, is simply this:
*You* taught me how to live again.

# Chapter 6

## Vanessa gets excited

I couldn't wait to tell Vanessa. I was tempted to call her when I finished work, but it was two in the morning and I couldn't be sure of a warm response. It would have to wait.

I slept like the dead. I tell you, there's nothing like stacking the old baked beans to guarantee uninterrupted Z's. I woke at midday and luxuriated for a while in the memory of my conversation with Jason. My little slip of the tongue had been a godsend. For all I know, I could have continued gibbering about soccer, getting absolutely nowhere. Clearly, Jason liked the direct approach. Good job I had blundered into it.

That set me thinking. Maybe he had called already. I leaped out of bed and threw on a blue T-shirt with a cartoon crocodile in a deck chair on the back (fashion icon, me) and raced into the kitchen. The Fridge was sitting at the table, drinking coffee. She obviously wasn't expecting me to appear at such a pace, because she spilled a fair amount down her front.

"My God, Calma," she said. "Is your bed on fire?"

"Has anyone called for me?"

"What?"

"Phone? You know, the lumpy device with buttons, over there on the wall?"

"How was your first shift at work?"

"Masterly. I'm on my way to becoming CEO of the entire organization. Has anyone called?"

"Like who?"

"Like anyone. Like someone saying, 'Hello, can I speak to Calma Harrison, please?' That sort of someone."

"No. Who were you expecting to call?"

"Me? No one. No one at all. Why would I be expecting someone to call? Nothing on the answering machine, then?"

The Fridge looked at me over the rim of her coffee cup. "What's going on, Calma?"

"I saw the poisoned dwarf at work last night."

"The poisoned dwarf?"

"You remember. Little runt, head like a cue ball, face like a baboon's bum. You used to be married to him. Goodness, how soon we forget!"

"What did he want?"

"To talk."

"And did you?"

"No. I rammed him in the gonads with a substantial warehouse cart and that seemed to stop the conversation dead in its tracks."

"Unfortunate."

"Yes. Where's a one-ton truck when you need it?"

I cut the banter and called Vanessa. I got her out of bed. Can you believe it? *She* hadn't been working until the small hours. She'd probably hit the sack at nine-thirty and I was still up before her! Her mum got her to the phone. Vanessa's voice was thick and heavy with sleep. Mind you, even at her most awake she does a remarkable impersonation of someone just roused from six months' intensive hibernation.

I arranged to go over to her house.

Brushing off further questions from the Fridge, I showered and slung on my new denim skirt and red EMILY THE STRANGE T-shirt. Yellow glasses and I was ready. Vanessa lived a few minutes' walk from my place, so I was in her front room before I could even build up a decent film of sweat.

Vanessa's mum was a person in a permanent state of frenzy. She looked as if she was expecting a homicidal maniac to appear out of the woodwork at any moment. Her eyes darted everywhere and her feet twitched in a fight-or-flight agony of indecision. Maybe that's why Vanessa turned out the way she did, as a reaction against parental influence. I have to say this about Vanessa: there's not much that gets under her skin. The world can be falling apart around her, and she still keeps calm. It's one of the things I like most about her.

"Hi, Mrs. Aldrick," I said cheerily.

She reacted like an SAS squadron had rappelled down the walls and crashed through the window. It was like cornering a wild jungle beast.

"Hello, Calma," she said finally. "Vanessa's in her bed-room."

And she scuttled off, possibly to cower in the corner of the garden or maybe do a little ironing. Mrs. Aldrick kept a tidy place. Even the cockroaches wiped their feet before they came into her house.

Vanessa was sitting up in bed, in the lotus position, her wrists balanced delicately on her knees, fingers making an O. Her eyes were closed in an annoying I'm-so-relaxed-even-the-corners-of-my-eyes-don't-crinkle-when-they're-shut fashion. I'd been in this situation before. Vanessa was so deep in her transcendental trance that nothing would rouse her until she was ready. Loud coughs, a low-flying jet plane, an earthquake measuring six on the Richter scale—none of these would have any effect. So I sat on the edge of the bed and waited.

Eventually Vanessa opened her eyes and let her breath out in one long, slow exhalation. I didn't say anything. I knew there was a routine we had to go through first. Vanessa contin-ued to take deep, deliberate breaths, her diaphragm swelling like that guy's in the first *Alien* movie just before something nasty erupted from his rib cage. A low hum issued from her nose. This was some kind of mantra. It might have been "om," but I don't have Vanessa's fluency in meditation-speak, so I can't swear to it. I continued to wait.

Finally, her eyes lost their hypnotic glaze, she shook her head slightly, and Vanessa was back on the plane of existence where she could communicate with the unenlightened. She brushed her long, fair hair back from her face, pale freckles framed by two straight, shining curtains.

"Hello, Calma," she intoned.

I say "intoned" not because I want to be artsy-fartsy, but because Vanessa's voice never expresses much in the way of emotion. It was like one of those computer-generated simulations of human speech that invests as much excitement into "Today is Sunday" as "Woohoo! I've won twenty-four million dollars in the lottery!" Vanessa's voice always gave the impression that communication was something she found tiring. You wouldn't be surprised if she had to take a nap after the exertion of a complete sentence.

"I've got a boyfriend," I blurted out.

Okay, this wasn't quite the way I had practiced breaking the news. I'd intended leading up to it gently, throwing it in casually when the opportunity arose.

(*"It's funny you should bring up refugee internment, Vanessa, because I was just saying to Jason yesterday . . . Jason? Haven't I mentioned Jason to you? Good heavens, mind like a sieve. He's just a guy who finds me irresistibly attractive. I've agreed to go out with him this week. It was easier to agree than listen to his blubbering and pleading. Anyway, he was gazing up at me adoringly—you know, drinking in every word—and I said, 'Jason, the thing about this government's policy on refugee status . . .' "*)

I hadn't meant to give the impression that a date with a guy was something totally unexpected, like the reappearance of the Tasmanian tiger. Blew that big-time. It was all I could do to stop myself bouncing up and down on her bed, clutching my hair in both hands, shrieking incoherently.

Vanessa raised one eyebrow two microns and I knew she was shocked to the core of her being.

"A boyfriend?" she said. "Why?"

"What do you mean, why?" I said. "What kind of a question is that? How about 'Who?' or 'Dish me the dirt, girlfriend'?"

"Hmmm," said Vanessa, uncurling her legs with the speed and elegance of a spreading flower. "Let's have a cup of dandelion tea and you can tell me about it."

It was a long sentence for Vanessa and it obviously took a lot out of her, because five minutes elapsed before we made it into the kitchen.

Mrs. Aldrick prepared tea and put out a tray of cheese, rice crackers and seedless grapes. I offered to help, but she twitched manically as if I'd suggested initiating a nuclear strike on North Korea, and scuttled off with little whimpers of anxiety. Vanessa and I sat at the kitchen table and picked at the food.

I ran through the events of the previous day, with considerable emphasis on the conversation with Jason. To be honest, I indulged in a certain amount of editing. I mean, would you admit to that embarrassing soccer stuff? So I cleaned up the story and recast it to some extent, so that I was a touch more charming and witty, ever so slightly more in control.

Okay. I told a pack of lies.

Vanessa listened. At least, I think she listened. She could

have fallen asleep, but I don't think so. She was nibbling on a cracker, slowly. It took ages to disappear. It was like watching the erosion of a sandstone cliff. Vanessa doesn't eat much, but then again she doesn't have to. That one cracker would balance out the calories she expends in an average day and still leave room for fat storage.

I finally finished my little tale, giving prominence to Jason's physical attractiveness, and waited for Vanessa's response. I didn't know what to expect. Vanessa had never shown any interest in boys and I didn't know if this was to conserve energy or because she genuinely didn't like them. The most reaction I had ever seen was when she curled a lip fractionally at the football-kicking drongos in the schoolyard. But where she stood on the issue of boy-girl romantic entanglements was a closed book. So I was curious.

"He'll want sex," she said finally.

"What?"

"Sex. He'll want it."

"Oh, my God," I yelled. "You can't be serious. Sex! Who'd have thought it? Boy meets girl, and the next thing you know sexual attraction is involved. What am I going to do? Get the Mace out! Call the vice squad now! Sex!"

Mrs. Aldrick poked her head around the door. It was probably the first time she had heard the word *sex* yelled in her kitchen and she wasn't responding well. But she disappeared quickly.

Vanessa continued to stare at me. She treated sarcasm

the same way she treated a snarling dog. If you ignored it, it generally lost interest and wandered away to urinate on a telephone pole.

"They're only interested in one thing," she said, unembarrassed by her lack of originality.

"Jason isn't," I replied. "He's interested in soccer as well."

Vanessa sniffed.

"Oh, come on, Nessa," I said. "You're behaving like a grandmother." I was tempted to tell her about the condom-buying geriatric but didn't think it would go down well. "I mean, what about your whole sixties thing? I thought you were into that era. Well, they invented free love. You couldn't sit next to someone on a bus in the sixties and not have sex with them. No one got any work done because they were at it continually. Rabbits were feeling sexually inadequate in comparison. Come on!"

"Just be careful. That's all I'm saying."

To be honest, Vanessa had taken the gloss off my news. I'd wanted a little enthusiasm and now I felt like I had gone to confession and needed to recite two hundred Hail Marys. Even a "That's nice" would have done. I felt cheated and resentful.

I made my excuses and left. I hadn't intended staying long anyway, on the grounds that it was unlikely I'd hear my phone ringing from a distance of half a mile. I plodded home in the blazing sun, but it felt like I had a small black cloud attached. Nothing gets under Vanessa's skin. She always keeps calm. It's one of the things that annoys me the most about her.

The Fridge had gone and hadn't left a note to say anyone

had called. I checked the answering machine. Nothing. I tried the caller ID function on the phone as well and drew a blank.

It was 2:33 p.m. precisely. No problem. I'd do some reading. There was no point just hanging around waiting for the phone to ring, like a complete loser. I wasn't one of those sad people who mope, dependent upon others for their state of well-being. No, I was a busy person with demands on my time. Things to see, people to do.

But what if Jason had lost my phone number and was even now desperately trying to track me down? Maybe he had been mugged on the way home from work and his wallet, with my number in it, had been snatched. Perhaps he was somewhere saying, "I don't care about the credit cards and the two hundred bucks, but Calma's phone number is an irreparable loss." Maybe he was frantic with anxiety.

Eventually, at 2:35 p.m., I called him.

We arranged to go to the movies on Friday.

I forgot to stay mad at Vanessa.

# Chapter 7

## Keeping the Fridge up to speed

*Dear Fridge,*

I am writing this slowly because I know you can't read fast.

It is spring and the sap is rising. I am not referring to your ex-husband, incidentally. No, I am merely identifying the season and its signifiers: primal juices are abundant within nature, new shoots appear, blossoms unfurl. So too beats the primeval rhythm within the human breast, a beat to which I am not immune. In short, dear Fridge, this Friday evening I am following the well-trodden path of romance, whereby a young English gentleman, the classically named Jason, with accompanying Greek god looks, will escort me to a place of entertainment and possibly thereafter to realms of amorous bliss.

Thought you should know.

Love,

*Calma*

*Dear Calma,*

About time you got a date.

Incidentally, it might be spring where your young man comes from, but in the tropics it's too bloody hot for rising sap, new shoots, or unfurling blossoms. Sorry to be practical.

Have a great time on Friday. Watch those primal juices. Haven't they told you about them in Health Education?

Love,

*The Fridge*

# Chapter 8

## Finding the Fridge is a fibber

The Fridge was up to no good.

Now, this might be news to you, but I have a reputation as an amateur sleuth. Not an undeserved one either, if you'll forgive me inserting my own trumpet and giving a resounding rendition. Call it a gift, but I can spot duplicity (what a brilliant word that is) from twenty miles without a road map. I can smell a lie. I can taste a half-truth. I'm allergic to deception. I'm part bloodhound. In fact, only last year I helped solve the mystery of the unmuzzled pit bull . . . but that's another story and I don't want to revisit it.

Anyway, it was but the work of a moment for me to piece the parts of the jigsaw together and come to the conclusion that the Fridge was telling me whoppers. However, the pieces of that jigsaw came in subtle ways. And the problem I've got is how best to tell you the details without boring you senseless.

You see, if I'm going to be honest, the separate events are not in themselves of stunning dramatic quality. Plus the evidence accumulated gradually, over days.

So . . . I've decided you are going to have to do some work as well. Don't worry, it's not physically demanding. All I ask is that when you see the word FastF™ (Calma Harrison, patent pending) on the page, then you mentally press the fast-forward button on an imaginary remote control. Listen, use a real remote control if it makes you feel better, but not much is going to happen unless you're reading this when the rest of the family is watching a movie, in which case you'll find your popularity suddenly plummets.

It's a narrative device I've just invented, where we can skip the dull bits of normal existence and focus on the relevant stuff. I can tell you're dubious, but give it a go. Okay?

Let's practice.

*Well, it's Sunday night and getting dark. The rain is coming down like stainless-steel rivets and the tree frogs are carrying on like foghorns. I think I'd better do that homework. . . .*
FastF™

*Slap me round the face with a wet fish! It's Monday morning and my homework's done. The sun is boiling the blacktop and . . .*

Get the general idea? Okay. Let's give it a go with "The Strange Case of the Dissembling Fridge."

I told you earlier that the Fridge was out when I got back from Vanessa's on Sunday afternoon. I didn't give it much thought. She's always out, doing one of her two jobs. She works in a supermarket in the next suburb. It's a better one than Crazi-Cheep. They've got two Muzak CDs and they can spell the name of the store properly. Positively upmarket. Anyway, she does strange shifts in the supermarket.

When she's not there, she's at her other place of employment—the casino on the Esplanade. She used to work in a pub but got tired of the relentless insults and sexual harassment. And that was just from the other employees. So now she deals cards for grim-faced tourists who, even when they win, look as happy as if she was performing a colonic irrigation on them. The hours are weird there too.

Look, all this is just background information. If I was wondering where the Fridge was on that Sunday afternoon, I probably assumed she was at one of those places. Actually, I wouldn't have given it a moment's thought. After all, I had arranged a date with Jason. I was basking in a mellow glow, almost certainly humming while skipping blithely through the garden, scattering rose petals. The Fridge was not high on my list of priorities.

There weren't even alarm bells when Mr. Moyd from the casino called. For a moment I thought it might have been Jason calling back, just to hear my voice, and I got to the phone before it had rung twice. Mr. Moyd, an American with an accent you could sharpen a cutthroat razor on, asked me to pass a message to the Fridge. It went something like: "Tail yer mom that aim shoor sorry thet she's failing seek too day. Ai hev gotten coveh for hair sheeft tonite, so she musn wurry. Send mah baist re-guards."

Even without the benefit of subtitles, I got the gist. The Fridge was crook and had the evening off. Selfish and preoccupied as I was, I forgot about it in an instant. . . .

FastF™

Monday afternoon and Jupiter must be in conjunction with Saturn or something, because when I get home from school, the Fridge is parked in the kitchen. Next to the fridge, actually. We pass a few pleasantries.

"How was school today, Calma?"

"Crap. How was work last night?"

"Ditto."

"You in again tonight?"

"Leaving in five minutes. There's a casserole in the oven."

"I'll take a shower first."

FastF™

I'm standing in the shower, trying to cover myself completely in soapsuds, when a small, niggling thought at the back of my mind bursts through to consciousness. Mr. Moyd. The message. What's going on?

FastF™

*　*　*

It's late at night and I can't concentrate on math. Actually, that's a normal state of affairs for me, but this time I have a reason. The Fridge told me she was at work last night, but Mr. Moyd specifically said she hadn't been in. If she chucked a sickie, then where did she go?

I call the casino. She isn't in. Reception tells me she has called in sick again and won't be in until Friday. I hang up and return to the math problem on my graphics calculator. It has something to do with box plots, statistical functions, and standard deviation distribution graphs. Don't worry. It doesn't make any sense to me either. Anyway, the only standard deviation I'm worried about is the one involving the Fridge.

FastF™

It's late Wednesday afternoon and the Fridge is leaving the house just as I'm coming in from school. She is carrying car keys and a vexed expression. I get between her and the driver's seat. I was tempted to leave a note but decided against it. If something funny is going on, I don't want to give her the chance to polish a lie. I want to look her in the eye.

"Where do you think you've been, young lady?"

Actually, I don't say that. I want to, mind. I want to stand there, hands on hips and a pissy look on my face, like I'm getting in serious preparation for parenthood.

"Mr. Moyd from the casino called on Sunday. He said you had called in sick. And you weren't in Monday night either. What's going on, Mum?"

The Fridge looks at me and I think I detect a shiftiness in

her eyes. It might be annoyance at running late, though. I can't be sure.

"Caught me ditching, Calma?" She is trying to lighten the tone, but I'm having none of it. I give her my steely gaze.

"Look," she says, "I had to work at the supermarket on Sunday and Monday. I'd double-booked myself, but I couldn't tell the casino that, could I? So I called in sick. Shoot me! Now I'm sorry, Calma, but I'm late and unless you get out of my way, I'll drop you with a karate chop to the neck."

It sounds reasonable. The explanation, that is, not the threat of mindless violence. I stand aside and she drives off. I feel easier in my mind.

FastF™

It is Friday evening and I am waiting outside the cinema for Jason. I'm tingly with nervousness, scanning the crowds of people, looking for his face. I am thirty minutes early and worried I'll seem too eager. I tried to be late. My brain had issued firm instructions to the rest of my body that a lateness of at least ten minutes was required, on the grounds that this would ensure Jason would be tingly with anticipation and scanning the crowds of passersby for *my* face. Unfortunately, the rest of my body had performed a bloodless coup and propelled itself to the cinema with unseemly haste.

I see the Fridge.

The cinema is part of a large shopping and entertainment complex. There are many restaurants and bars. I catch a glimpse of a woman's face as she enters a restaurant. She has her back to me and is partly obscured by passing traffic. But she turns her face briefly to the side and smiles at someone next to her. I can't see who it is. It is over in a flash, a fraction of a second, a single frame in the spool of time. Too quick to be sure.

But I *am* sure. It's the Fridge.

I move toward the restaurant, but Jason separates from a crowd and I stop. It wouldn't take much to go over and check, peer in through the window, but suddenly I'm scared of knowledge and its implications. I smile at Jason and we collect our tickets.

FastF™

"Did you have fun last night?" says the Fridge. "And why are you wearing that towel around your head?"

It is Saturday morning and I'm picking at a round of toast. The Fridge is drinking coffee.

"Yeah, great," I reply, ignoring her last question. "How was work?"

"Oh, you know. Work is work. Nothing to write home about. Tell me about your evening."

But I don't. Not really. My heart isn't in it.

I want to know why she is lying to me but don't have the courage to ask. I'm not sure if I can handle the truth.

ReWND™

I forgot to tell you about the rewind function, didn't I? Well, it's a logical extension, after all. I've skipped over some pretty important stuff, not the least being the big date with Jason, and we've got to engage in some literary time travel if we want to get it all in.

Anyway, wait until you get to the ReCRD™ button. Trust me. It'll blow your mind.

# Chapter 9

## Just your average week

Actually, when I think about it, I'm not sure I want to go over the events of the week. If I'm honest, it wasn't the best week I've ever experienced. Not that anything went *terminally* wrong, you understand. But not a whole lot went right, either.

You know I said I had missed some important stuff and that's why we had to go back in time? That's not strictly true. Sorry. It was a cheap narrative device to keep you focused. Of course, the date with Jason was interesting and I will give you a full run-down later. But the rest of the week was not high on drama, so yes, I misled you. I apologize. Believe me when I say I feel better for having got that off my chest.

I'll start with Vanessa.

You'll remember I left Vanessa's house on Sunday in a state of simmering resentment at her lukewarm reaction to my romantic liaison with Jason. You might also recall that by the time I had finished on the phone with Jason, I had mellowed.

It's difficult to stay mad at someone when you're feeling particularly optimistic, and anyway, Vanessa is too calm. She dilutes drama. If she had been the first person on the moon, she'd have yawned through it all. Instead of "This is one small step for a man, but a giant leap for mankind," we'd have "Like, is there any *point* to mankind?" for posterity to contemplate.

So I went to school prepared, eager even, to forgive and forget. At lunchtime Vanessa was already on the benches outside the canteen when I rocked up. She was chipping away at a banana and staring off into the middle distance, pondering the mysteries of the universe. I plopped myself down beside her.

I'd given this some thought. I wasn't going to mention Jason. I was going to be completely normal, chatting away as usual. If she had a problem with my love life, and I couldn't understand why she should, then I wasn't going to give her any opportunities to articulate it. A good plan, I thought. Unfortunately, it was a doomed one.

"Hey ho, Vanessa," I said in a frighteningly cheerful voice. "Here we are again. It's Monday morning and the week stretches before us like a pitted path to nowhere. Tell me, why are two urbane sophisticates like us marking time in this academic wasteland when we could be out in the real world amassing personal fortunes and making indelible marks upon history?"

Not an aggressive opening statement, I think you will admit.

"I'm surprised you bother to talk to me," Vanessa replied.

"What?" I said. Sometimes I fluctuate wildly between a flood of words and a dribble. This time I was just stunned.

"Nothing," she said, keeping her head turned from me.

"Hang on," I said. I wasn't going to let this go. "What do you mean, bother to talk? Why wouldn't I talk to you?"

Vanessa squirmed. She kept her head at an angle so I couldn't make eye contact, shutting me out.

"Now that you've got a boyfriend," she said, "I figured you'd find me dull company."

I laughed. I couldn't help it. She sounded so childish, like we were both six years old. Maybe I should have left it at that, possibly put my arm around her shoulders to comfort her. But it was absurd. I've never been good at dealing with immaturity and I've also got an alarming tendency to speak my mind regardless of the consequences.

I'm not proud of this. It's just the way it is.

"Have you completely lost it, Vanessa?" I said. "What are you on about? Do you really think that because I've got a date with a guy—he's not even my boyfriend, damn it—it diminishes you as a human being? Are you so insecure you can't bear for me to have relationships with other people? What do you want me to do? Stop speaking to anyone else, to protect your jealous possessiveness? We are not in preschool, Vanessa. You're being pathetic."

She turned toward me and I saw her eyes were filled with tears. Her face crumpled. I was shocked. It was so rare that Vanessa showed any emotion at all and now her whole being was drenched in it. And for what? For nothing.

"Thanks," she said, her voice strangled and tight with feeling. "Childish? I see. I've never been good enough for you and your smart talk. No one is good enough for Calma Harrison. It's not all about you, bloody big-shot Calma. No one wants to be your friend because you pride yourself on making people feel small and worthless. Didn't you ever wonder why the only friend you've ever managed to keep was a mindless dickhead? That Kiffing boy. He made you feel really superior, didn't he?"

It felt, literally, as if someone had smacked me across the face. I don't know where the tears came from. It's a cliché, I know, but it was like an internal tap had opened. My chest felt as if a massive weight had me pinned. I couldn't breathe. For once I could find no words. Even my brain was paralyzed. I watched in a daze as Vanessa threw down the remains of her banana and stormed off. Then, with a dark, malevolent surge, the anger swelled within me and I was on my feet.

I yelled at her retreating back.

"And what the hell do you know, Vanessa? About me, about Kiffo, about anything?" She didn't stop. "Fuck you, Vanessa. *Fuck you!*"

I can't stand immaturity in others, but I have a surprisingly high tolerance of it in myself. Strange, isn't it?

If nothing else, I had the complete attention of every student within a hundred yards. Not that I cared. I also had the undivided attention of Mr. Haubrick, a teacher on yard duty. I spent the rest of the day in the office of the assistant principal for student welfare, where I continued to cry as if I was never going to stop. I refused to talk about Kiffo, though she tried to draw me out. I'm not going to tell you, either. I'm not in the mood. Sorry.

Remember I said earlier that the week wasn't high on drama? Okay, that was a fib as well. I've told you before and I'll tell you again: all narrators are unreliable, but some are more unreliable than others.

Then again, maybe I'm too smart for my own good.

I worked at Crazi-Cheep on Wednesday evening. It wasn't my normal shift. In fact, I had told them I could only work weekends because I didn't want anything that would interfere with schoolwork. I was forceful about that. Under no circumstances could I work Monday to Thursday. Non-negotiable. Set in stone. Don't even ask.

So they called me late Wednesday afternoon and I said yes.

There was an emergency. Three employees had called in sick with subacute pulmonary carcinoma of the clack, or something. Maybe it was flu. Maybe they wanted to wander around the riverfront and lie to their children about it. Anyway, the store was desperate and would I, just this once . . .

I wasn't doing anything anyway. The Fridge was out (who knew where) and I was torn between knocking my head against probability theory or feeling depressed over the things Vanessa had said. Perhaps paid employment would take me out of myself. Perhaps there would just be me and Jason in the store.

He wasn't in and I worried for a while if he had succumbed to the mystery clack ailment, and if so, whether it would have cleared up by Friday.

Candy was in, though. I got the impression she never took a night off sick, possibly because no self-respecting virus would touch her. She looked at me as if I was something nasty left over in the mother-baby diaper-changing facility (I wanted them to rename it Crazi-Krap but didn't think it was worth suggesting to management). Or rather, she nearly looked at me. Her eyes slid over the fluorescent lighting as she explained the mysteries of register rolls, scanning procedures, and refund policies.

I was going to work the register!

So much for the theory that operating the checkout was up there with cardiac bypass operations in terms of complexity and experience required. A few people got sick and they threw in a complete novice. I don't know what they would have done if I hadn't been able to work—probably kidnapped a toddler from the parking lot and stuck him in a high chair at the register.

Anyway, it didn't seem complicated. Get the bar code in line with the scanner and away you go. I reckoned I could do that without burning out too many neurons. Candy wandered off to hone her gum-chewing skills at the customer service desk and I was left in charge of checkout six. It was the only one in operation. I had been hoping that all the carts laden with tricky items would miraculously line up at another register and I would be left with the handbaskets containing one item. With one checkout in operation, this seemed an unlikely scenario.

My first customer was all right. She *did* have a handbasket and there were only a few items in it. Now, I hadn't had any specific training, but I knew what to do. I fixed her with a dazzling smile, like she was a long-lost relative.

"And how are you this fine evening?" I said. It was difficult to enunciate properly while giving her the full range of my teeth, so it might have come out garbled. She certainly seemed startled, possibly at my exuberance, possibly at being confronted by a practicing ventriloquist, but she recovered quickly.

"I'm great, thank you. And you?"

"Couldn't be better." Actually, it came out as "Couldn-gee-getta," but I think she caught my drift. Grinning like a lunatic, I scanned her five items without faltering once, and rang up the total.

"That'll be four thousand, four hundred, and twenty-five dollars and forty cents, please," I said happily.

"Pardon?" she said.

"We take all major credit cards," I said.

She laughed. "I think you've made a mistake."

I couldn't fault her logic. I'd hoped she wouldn't notice, but I guess that was always going to be a long shot. I pressed a buzzer and a red lamp lit up above my checkout—useful if you've got twenty registers in operation but a bit redundant in this instance. Not difficult to spot the loser.

Candy meandered over and I explained the slight discrepancy. She tut-tutted without breaking her chewing rhythm and used the key around her neck to open my register.

"I do apologize, madam," Candy said to the customer. "She's new."

"*She?*" The woman's mouth twisted slightly. "You mean Calma? No need to apologize. A small mistake."

Candy grunted. I could tell she was disappointed. She was

clearly hoping the two of them could have a full and frank discussion of my customer-care shortcomings. Instead, she copped a put-down. It's good to savor moments like those and my smile widened. I could nearly suck my own ears. Candy canceled the transaction and slunk off without another word. I rang up the purchases again.

"You have qualified, madam, for a discount of nearly four and a half thousand dollars," I said, "for being one of the few people in the world to pronounce my name correctly." I pointed to the badge on my blouse. "Most say, 'Kal-ma,' when of course it's 'Kar-mer.' "

She laughed and it lit up her whole face. There are some people who exude an air of good humor, who give the impression that little, if anything, will stop them seeing the funny side of things. She was one of those. I warmed to her instantly.

"Calma," she said, "thank you. You have brightened my evening."

I could hear her laughing as she left the store.

The rest of the shift, believe it or not, went by with scarcely a hiccup. Okay, there were one or two small mistakes, but I sorted them out myself. Thankfully we weren't busy. I don't know where pensioners go on a Wednesday—bingo? mud wrestling? the over-eighty leapfrog national championships?—but they steered clear of Crazi-Cheep and I was grateful for that. I even managed to get in some thinking about Vanessa.

I knew she was right. Partly, anyway. I can be a smart-arse (does this come as a great shock to you?), but I have never tried to humiliate someone for the hell of it. And Vanessa seemed to be implying that I got a kick out of putting people down. Is that what others thought about me? I'm not a bitch. Honest. Not deliberately. Anyway, should I worry how others perceive me? It was Kiffo who taught me that changing your personality and behavior to suit other people's perceptions was wrong. But Vanessa worried me.

Why had she reacted so angrily? I couldn't understand it. She must have been suffering in some way, but the origin of the pain was a mystery. After my raw hurt subsided, I saw Vanessa's reaction for what it was—a cry for help. She had lashed out blindly and I should have felt angry if she *hadn't* used me as a target. What are friends for, after all? I made up my mind to go to her house at the earliest opportunity and talk.

She could be noncommunicative and downright strange, but Vanessa was my friend. I'm a little strange myself, if the truth be known.

The only other thing worth mentioning about my shift was that my father turned up at about eleven o'clock. I noticed him out of the corner of my eye, much the way you do when a rodent scuttles out of the wardrobe and disappears under the bed. (Look, it might not have happened to you, but you probably live somewhere where wildlife have the decency to observe negotiated boundaries.)

Anyway, he skittered among the aisles, pausing occasionally to scan the shelves. I wasn't fooled, though. He was giving me the once-over. Either that or there was something fascinating about the pan scourer section.

I ignored him and he disappeared. If only it could be that easy all the time! Certainly he didn't buy anything. When you're the only checkout operator, you notice stuff like that. It made me uneasy, though. When I left the store at midnight and walked the short distance home, I kept glancing over my shoulder. I had a horrible feeling someone was following. Once I thought I saw a shadow move when all the other shadows remained fixed. I stopped in the middle of the street and focused on using my peripheral vision, but I couldn't see anything.

It must have been my imagination.

I went round to Vanessa's house straight after school on Thursday. She had been avoiding me during the day and I wanted to defuse the tension.

Mrs. Aldrick opened the door in the manner of one expecting an advance party of invading aliens from Alpha Centauri, showed me into the front room, and disappeared in a flurry of rolling eyeballs. Vanessa was curled up on the sofa, watching something appalling on the TV. It was one of those soap operas where everyone is young, physically irresistible, morally unscrupulous, and emotionally screwed.

Scene 37

*Interior. Daytime. Vanessa's front room. Tasteful art is on the walls, potted plants with gleaming leaves stand in corners, and there is no hint of dirt anywhere. It looks like a room fumigated regularly by people in white coats and breathing apparatus. You could perform open-heart surgery on the dining table with complete confidence (see next episode).*

*Vanessa Aldrick, seventeen, is lying on the sofa. She is dressed in flowing robes of pure white that drape elegantly over slender limbs. Her hair, a pale waterfall, catches the light.*

*Enter Calma Harrison. She radiates good health. Her long, muscular, tanned legs are perfectly complemented by an immaculately tailored designer dress. Her bust heaves dramatically, threatening to explode out of the confining material and concuss a cameraman. When she smiles, impossibly white teeth flash like a solar flare.*

*She stands in front of Vanessa, one beautifully manicured hand on hip, the other running through the silk of her hair.*

*Calma: Nessa. You were right about Jason all along. He has been two-timing me with Charlene.*

*Nessa: That girl who is so attractive she makes us seem like the rear end of a constipated Rottweiler?*

*Calma: The very same. I found out tonight when he crashed his sports car (with her in it) into the coffee shop, killing four extras, ruining the special of the day and turning Tammy into a paraplegic.*

*Nessa: Tammy? The champion surfer with the honed body of an Olympic athlete and flawless makeup?*

*Calma: The very same.*

Vanessa and I talked. I apologized for swearing at her. She apologized for what she had said about Kiffo.

On the surface, we were okay again. But I wasn't satisfied. Vanessa was hiding something. I mean, it was fine that she recognized her overreaction, but she didn't offer any explanation for it. And there had to be something more. The difficulty would be getting it out of her—as you must have gleaned by now, Vanessa isn't the best communicator in the world. It was a problem.

I didn't have time that afternoon, so I filed the dilemma away for future reference. You see, I'd made an appointment at the hairdresser's for five o'clock and I didn't want to be late. I was overdue for a trim. My hair had been bothering me for some time. It had nothing to do with my date on Friday, you understand.

As it turned out, I wish I'd stayed with Vanessa and watched the rest of the soap opera.

# Chapter 10

## Just your average hairdo

I don't know how you are positioned on the feminist spectrum, but let me present you with a scenario. You are thinking of going to the hairdresser's to prepare for a date. Part of you is disturbed by this. You examine your motives and see if they stand up to rational scrutiny. Which of the following do you most identify with?

a) Going on a date should not compromise your standards. Trying to impress a guy with good grooming is a sad indictment of your insecurity. It is better to turn up exactly as you are, warts and all, and if he is not impressed, then he is a shallow individual not worthy of your attention in the first place.

b) It is entirely understandable to want to make an impression. If a trip to the local dump is normally preceded by ensuring you are clean and tidy, then a social engagement would obviously justify greater effort.

This would include paying attention to hair, makeup, and outfit. Not to do so would be artificial. What's the alternative? Not showering, and dressing in soiled shorts and ripped T-shirt with bird's-nest hair?

c) You might as well go whole hog—hairdo, manicure, pedicure, liposuction, Botox, facelift, nose job, new outfit from Versace, and sufficient makeup to cement a stone wall. Then leave half your brain cells at home and simply giggle and clutch the guy's arm from time to time.

It seemed to me that the second option was the mature and considered choice. So on Wednesday afternoon, before I went to work, I looked up hairdressers in the Yellow Pages.

I decided I wouldn't go to my usual place. Don't get me wrong. It was a fine establishment and Cheryl, my hairdresser, was competent at lopping off split ends while engaging in uninspiring conversation about the weather. I just felt she was more of an artisan than an artist.

I also didn't want to go to places that used puns in their business name. You know, things like The Final Cut or Hair Today. Don't ask me why. Oh, go on. Ask me why. They bloody annoy me, that's why. I refuse to hand over money to someone who thinks a weak pun is a brilliant marketing ploy. And as for anything with a *z* in it—Cutz, Endz—well, I wouldn't advocate firebombing under any circumstances, but I understand how someone might feel it was the only solution.

In the end I decided to give Alessandro's a go. I called for an appointment. It sounded expensive. You can tell these things from the receptionist's tone of voice. The trouble is, you can't ask about price on the phone, can you? I'm not sure why. It's an immutable law, like gravity or something.

After I left Vanessa's house, I took a bus straight to the mall. Alessandro's was next to fashion outlets that charged three hundred bucks for a miniskirt. Alessandro's was impressive. Black marble, a tasteful sign, spotlighting, no price list in the window. I felt inadequate just entering the place.

The receptionist gave me the once-over and didn't appear impressed. Maybe I should have left then. I can't stand people who think they're doing you a favor by accepting your business. The receptionist was stick-thin, dressed in black, and sporting a hairdo that stuck out at crazy angles. Undoubtedly it was the height of fashion. I fronted up to the counter and gave my name. She scanned the appointment book and seemed disappointed to find I had indeed booked.

The hairdresser came over and gave me the same look the receptionist did. "What would you like done?" she said, studying my hair. I can't be sure, but I think I detected a lip curling fractionally.

I'm fine in most social situations. I can talk intelligently to people. But hairdressers intimidate me. I suddenly find myself nervous and tongue-tied, as if I am not qualified to talk about my own hair.

"Well, I don't know, really," I said, not making the most confident start to the consultation. "A trim, I suppose. Get rid of the split ends and style it. Whatever you think." I hated myself as soon as I made that last remark.

The hairdresser examined my hair more closely.

"We might be able to do something," she said grudgingly, as if I'd asked her to weave a Persian carpet out of the fluff that gets stuck in the filters of tumble dryers. "Follow me, please."

The salon was plush, I must say. There were Aboriginal paintings on the walls, the lighting was discreet, and there was more stainless-steel gadgetry dotted about than you'd find in an average operating room. I started to really worry about cost. If push came to shove, I suppose I could have offered to sweep up hair to pay the bill, but I suspected I would have to accumulate enough to occupy a landfill site. I decided to worry about it later.

It was great at first. I had to put my glasses down on a counter, which meant the Aboriginal art became decidedly more abstract, at least from my perspective. Then I leaned back in a soft leather chair and an apprentice washed my hair and massaged my scalp. There's nothing like having someone else washing your hair. It takes you back to your childhood, when your mum used to lather your head into a frenzy. All I needed was a rubber duck to play with afterward and I would have been a happy girl.

When she had made my hair squeaky, I was led back to a seat in front of a mirror and the hairdresser combed my hair, occasionally lifting a portion off to the side, for reasons best known to herself. Certainly she didn't keep me informed of her progress. I couldn't see what she was doing. Without my glasses I have the visual acuity of a fruit bat. But there was plenty of prodding going on. I gazed impassively at the blurred reflection in the mirror. Finally she spoke.

"Who usually does your hair?" she said.

I told her and she grunted. I got the distinct impression she looked upon Cheryl in much the same way a brain surgeon would look upon a faith healer.

"Well," she continued, "your hair is a challenge. It's in appalling condition and the amateurish cuts you've had in the past mean there are limits to what I can do. I think it would be best if we started from scratch. I suggest we take a fair amount off the length . . . to about here." She was showing me in the mirror, but I got only the haziest notion of what she meant. "Then I can style it, so it follows the curve of your cheekbones. Like this." Again I squinted and again came up blank. "Does that sound all right?"

Now, tell me. What should you say under these circumstances? I mean, I know I hadn't been insulted personally, but it's difficult to keep your composure when someone is implying your hair is beneath contempt.

"Fine," I said.

I don't know if this has happened to you. If it hasn't, you'll have to trust me. There is a defining moment in a hairdresser's when you know, absolutely and unequivocally, that a disaster is occurring. It comes with the first snip of scissors just below your left ear and the sense of hair falling. Lots of hair. Hair that can never be returned. Hair today, gone forever.

The worst part is that you know a scream of "Stop!" is going to achieve nothing, except possibly a coronary for your hairdresser.

I went rigid with terror. Sweat glistened on my forehead. The spawn-of-Satan hairdresser carried on blithely snipping, huge swathes of hair flying around manically. My head was getting lighter, literally and metaphorically. In the end I shut my eyes. I resisted the urge to stick my thumb in my mouth and start sucking, but it was difficult.

The rest of the procedure was a blur. The snipping and slicing seemed to go on forever. Then there was a vigorous massage of the scalp with something greasy and a finale with a hair dryer and comb. Eventually, she declared she was done. I stood up and put on my glasses.

It's not often I've nearly lost control of my bladder, but this was touch-and-go. I looked in the mirror and Gollum in a toupee looked back. We regarded each other suspiciously for a moment before I was led to reception and presented with a bill for $110. Under other circumstances, I would have laughed derisively. This time I handed over my credit card meekly. The small part of my brain still functioning noted, in a calm and distant fashion, that this completely wiped out my checking account. I clutched the receipt, gathered up my bag, and went out into the mall.

I stood for a moment, hoping to see a bus I could throw myself under. Unfortunately, it was a mall.

Then, at my bleakest moment, I saw it. The solution. The only solution. The final solution.

I hurried across before the stall closed. I was the last customer. Ten minutes later, it was done. The Leukemia Foundation gave me a bandanna, which was a blessing, and heartfelt congratulations for doing my bit for those less fortunate than myself. I told them I'd get the money from my sponsors as soon as I could and drop the cash off at their main office.

I examined myself in a shop window. Even though you could stick two fingers up my nose and use me for a bowling ball, it was an improvement. I tied the bandanna around my completely shaved head and headed for the bus stop.

# Chapter 11

A reflection on the positives in life, after mature consideration

# Chapter 12

## Just your average date, part one

Here's another poser.

You have secured a date with a young man who makes Orlando Bloom look like the dog's dinner. Unfortunately, a deranged hairdresser has viciously attacked your head, necessitating a drastic solution that has left you doing an uncanny impersonation of a potato. You put on your glasses and look in a mirror. Ears stick out of a shiny globe, like handles on a hardboiled egg. If you went out on a sunny day, you'd dazzle the pilots of passing aircraft, precipitating a major catastrophe. What are you going to do?

Do you cancel the date or go ahead and hope he doesn't mind being seen in public with a bespectacled skinhead?

I tried other options. I went into the Fridge's wardrobe while she was out and found a blond wig. I had no idea why she owned one. Possibly it was a remnant from some ghastly costume party. You couldn't describe it as a top-of-the-line accessory. It had the consistency of freeze-dried straw and contained enough static electricity to run a small appliance. I put it on.

I looked like Goldilocks with breast implants.

I decided to call Jason and call the whole thing off. I mean, what choice did I have? Maybe I could rearrange it for three months' time, when I'd look as if I was at least a candidate for the human race. I'd even called the number—my finger was poised over the last digit—when I thought again.

If I gave him the elbow now, there was no chance of re-claiming the situation. There were probably dozens of girls waiting in the wings to snap him up. Girls with washboard stomachs, master's degrees in soccer administration, tiny halter tops, and long flowing hair that shimmered sexily as they walked. No. Jason was a once-in-a-lifetime opportunity.

I replaced the handset.

So what if I had a head like an inflated marble? There's more to attractiveness than the physical. I had a personality. I could be warm, charming, witty. Why should I prejudge Jason, compartmentalize him as a shallow chauvinist, when all the time he could be searching for an intelligent soul mate? For all I knew he was a closet Buddhist. To hell with it. I'd go. I knew I'd regret it if I didn't.

I felt better once I'd made the decision, so I locked myself in my bedroom and cried for two hours.

I was buggered if I was going to school, though.

Thursday evening wasn't too bad. I stayed in, watching

Discovery while simultaneously trying to decipher the arcane mysteries of probability theory. As far as I understood it, the probability of waking up the next morning with a full head of hair was zero, while the probability of Jason dropping me like a handful of warm diarrhea was approaching one. While these amusing notions passed through my head, I kept one eye on the driveway. If the Fridge turned up, I could be in my bedroom before her key hit the front door. I needn't have worried. Once more, the Fridge was missing in action. By the time I hit the sack at eleven o'clock, she still wasn't home.

I slept surprisingly well and woke refreshed. For a moment or two, I had difficulty believing my recollections of the previous day and had to check myself out in the mirror. The early morning light glinted off my pate and made intricate patterns on the ceiling. The birds stopped singing. I had the cranial characteristics of a Tibetan monk.

I wrapped my head in a towel (at least I was still thinking rationally and strategically) and slipped downstairs into the kitchen. The Fridge was home—the car was parked in the driveway—but there was no sign of her. Probably still sleeping. I made toast and thought about rubbing Vegemite on my scalp, but decided against it. It probably wouldn't do anything and I'd spend the day with a cloud of flies buzzing around my head. Or, worse, stuck to it.

Keeping my voice quiet, I called school and told them I wouldn't be in on account of a severe inflammation of the clack picked up at work. Then I pinned a note to the Fridge on the fridge, telling her I wasn't feeling crash-hot and needed to catch up on sleep. I padded back up the stairs and into my bedroom, where the day stretched out interminably before me. At least I'd have time to plan what I was going to wear.

I was surprised to discover my resolution to go ahead with the date hadn't diminished overnight. If anything, all remaining doubts had vanished. If Jason was the kind of guy to be put off by someone who'd shaved her head for charity, then he could shove his impeccably fine features where the sun don't shine. This would be a test. A test of his inner beauty. What did I have to lose?

This line of thought cheered me immensely and I turned my mind to matters of apparel. One thing was clear. I couldn't wear any of my glasses. I tried them all, believe me. But it was impossible.

The kind of glasses I like are bold. Well, not so much bold as downright arrogant. And they wouldn't work. Stick a brightly colored pair of specs on a cantaloupe if you don't believe me. So this left one option. A few years previously, I had tried contact lenses. I think I was going through a self-conscious stage before I discovered that the best way of overcoming embarrassment at wearing glasses was to make them a feature. A sort of in-your-face, stuff-you-if-you-don't-like-'em, I-couldn't-give-a-rat's approach.

Actually, this discovery was prompted by the physical pain involved with contact lenses. Getting the buggers in was torture. It was like sticking thumbtacks into your eyeballs. And every time I blinked I felt like confessing to crimes I hadn't committed.

I still had the contact lenses and the expensive gunk they came in. It was time to give them another go.

I perched in front of the mirror, one lens balanced delicately on an index finger, the fingers of the other hand prying my left eyelid open, tongue sticking out the corner of my mouth in concentration. Then it was simply a case of bringing the lens onto the surface of the eyeball in one smooth, decisive action. Unfortunately, due to the reflex action that in prehistoric times was invaluable in preserving my forebears' eyesight, I would blink at the critical moment, spinning the lens off to a corner of the bedroom, where it would disappear into the carpet. Then I'd spend half an hour finding the bloody thing, cleaning it, and going through the whole process again.

I spent the entire morning doing this before I managed to get both lenses in. Feeling proud, I stood in front of the mirror and examined the results. True, I couldn't see much because my eyes were streaming with tears, but it didn't seem too bad. I thought the swelling would probably subside by the time I met Jason.

That left my clothes. I could go for the bold approach. Trousers, waistcoat, maybe even a tie. Too sexually ambiguous, I decided. Or there was the feminine angle—print dress with soft, flowing lines, complemented with chunky Doc Martens. My head could act as another stylistic counterpoint at the other end. Too schizophrenic? And what about my head itself? Should I go out bareheaded, scalp gleaming in the light of streetlights, or would a scarf be better? Maybe a floppy hat?

Could I keep it on throughout the movie? Dubious. With my luck, I'd sit in front of a dwarf and be forced to remove it. No, there was no way I could go the entire evening without Jason finding out. What if he tried to run his hands through my hair during the film? I could imagine his scream when he discovered he was fondling a boulder.

I had made little headway on the thorny problem of appropriate dress when I heard the Fridge leave, about three-thirty. The front door slammed and there was a crunch of tires on gravel. I waited ten minutes before I went downstairs. I'd seen too many films where an unsuspecting bald heroine had been caught by sneaky decoys like that.

I got to the front room and the phone rang. It was Candy from Crazi-Cheep.

"Hello, Calma?" she said. "I was wondering if you could work tonight. We're short-staffed again."

"I can't, Candy," I replied. "I've got a bone in my leg."

There was a five-second pause.

"I'm sorry to hear that," she said. "Hope you're better soon."

I put the phone down and the doorbell rang. Typical, I thought. For hours the Fridge is home and open to the public and nothing happens. As soon as she leaves, it's open house. I snuck over to the curtains. I might have mentioned already that the view from the window is not perfect, but this time I was lucky. Swirling paisley material and a glimpse of long blond hair told me Vanessa was at the door.

I didn't hesitate. I unwrapped the towel from my head,

raced to the front door, opened it sharply, and went, "Boo!" Vanessa screamed. The look on her face was priceless. I was making a habit of getting a reaction out of Nessa these days. She stood stock still for a moment, eyes glazed, her mouth describing a perfect little O. If I'd tapped her forehead with my finger, she'd have gone over like a felled tree.

"Wassup, Nessa?" I said. "Care to come in and give my skull a buff and polish?"

And then she started to laugh. Really laugh. Laugh in a way I'd never heard from Vanessa before, as if an internal barrier had been breached and what was bubbling up was fresh, pure, unstoppable. I couldn't help myself. I laughed too, bent double, tears running down my face and threatening to wash my contact lenses onto the welcome mat. We held on to each other, lungs struggling to get air, pain like a sharp band along my side. Laughing.

**Fact File**

*Common name:* Vanessa Aldrick

*Scientific name: Hippius noncommunicado*

*Habitat:* This creature spends most of its time asleep to conserve energy. Can occasionally be seen searching through sad racks of clothing in secondhand shops or in the folk section of record stores.

*Mating habits:* Unknown. Scientific studies are proceeding.

*Appearance:* Brightly colored, the *Hippius noncommunicado* is nonetheless a retiring creature. Favors loose-flowing, garish plumage and is renowned for its inability to evolve.

*Distinguishing characteristics:* Normally unresponsive to human contact, but is loyal and supportive if treated with patience and kindness.

*Status:* Possesses hidden depths while appearing barely sentient.

Sometimes you think you've got someone pinned down and classified and then they leap up and surprise you.

Vanessa came into the house and disappeared off to the toilet, pleading a severely weakened bladder. I heard her giggling from the front room. I wiped the tears from my eyes and a thought skittered across my mind. Was this why I liked Vanessa? Because I could sometimes provoke such reactions from her, though her natural tendency was toward gloominess? Was she merely a mirror I held up to my own wit? It was an uncomfortable thought and I put it to one side. It occurred to me I was doing that a lot recently, postponing stuff. Was I a procrastinator? I'd think about it tomorrow.

When Nessa came out, we sat on the couch and I told her about my disastrous trip to the hairdresser. I didn't even have to exaggerate for comic effect. The truth was bizarre enough. I set her off laughing again. I liked it when Vanessa laughed. She got all these sparks in her eyes. Her smile injected her face with life. She looked beautiful.

It was a pity she looked like that so rarely. Nonetheless, I reflected, she had come a long way since primary school, when a smile from Nessa coincided with the appearance of Halley's comet. I liked to think I'd helped her in that regard. Since we'd become friends she smiled much more frequently. Vanessa had also been disastrously accident-prone. She missed heaps of days from school and would come in with bandages and Band-Aids up her arms. Fell off her bike, slipped in the shower. But not since we'd teamed up. I wasn't sure how to put this down to my influence, but I was prepared to accept the credit.

"Listen," she said after I finished the sad and sorry tale of my misadventures in grooming. "I'm going to the movies tonight. I swear to God I'm not going to check out Justin."

"Jason," I said.

"Whatever. I'm spending the weekend with Dad and I don't want to get to his house too early. I need to kill some time."

Nessa, like me, was in a single-parent household. Unlike me, however, she had a father who showed interest, so every month she'd spend a weekend with him. I got the impression she wasn't keen on it. She never talked about him, for example. Mind you, she rarely talked about anything, so I suppose that wasn't a clinching argument. It was just a feeling I had.

"Do you want to come with Jason and me?" I asked.

Her eyes widened in surprise.

"No," she said. "Not at all. I just told you in case you spotted me and thought I was spying on you."

"Good," I said. "I wasn't going to invite you, anyway."

I smiled when I said it, though, and she knew I was joking. Her eyes sparked briefly.

"Just as well you mentioned it, however," I continued. "You're right. I might have come to the wrong conclusion if I'd seen you in the next row hiding behind a supersized popcorn."

Vanessa left about ten minutes later. She had to pack for her weekend stay. She touched me on the arm when we got to the front door.

"I hope you have a great time tonight, Calma," she said. "Really. And I'm sorry I was such a loser when you told me."

"Hey," I said. "Forget it. And give me a hug."

In the end, I decided on a simple outfit. Long blue fisherman's pants, a white halter-neck top I had been saving for a special occasion, and black leather flip flops. I checked in the mirror and was pleased with what I saw. Mind you, what I could see wasn't crystal clear. Those damn contact lenses were still giving me grief.

Oh, and I wore a dark, floppy hat. Very floppy. Completely spineless. The hat, not me. Well, me as well, when I come to think about it.

I set off very early for the date. I hadn't intended to. My brain had issued firm instructions to the rest of my body that a lateness of at least ten minutes was required, on the grounds that this would ensure Jason would be tingly with anticipation, scanning the crowds of passersby for my face.

FastF™

I saw the Fridge.

FastF™

It was all over in a flash, a fraction of a second, a single frame in the spool of time. Too quick to be sure.

But I *was* sure. It was the Fridge.

I moved towards the restaurant, but Jason separated from a crowd and I stopped. It wouldn't have taken much to go over and check, peer in through the window at the customers, but suddenly I was scared of knowledge and its implications. I smiled at Jason and we collected our tickets.

**From:** Miss Moss <moss.aj@lotis.edu.au>
**To:** Calma Harrison <harrison.c@lotis.edu.au>
**Subject:** Sonnet

---

Calma,

I'd like you to try a Shakespearean sonnet! As you know, the sonnet form is (essentially) fourteen lines of iambic pentameter, with a specific rhyme scheme. The Shakespearean form has a rhyme scheme of *ababcdcdefefgg*—in other words, you finish with a rhyming couplet. Have a look at Shakespeare's sonnets—you will already be familiar with a good number, like sonnet 18, "Shall I compare thee to a summer's day"—but don't be put off. I'm not expecting work of his standards!

Write about a person who is, or was, important to you (we might as well keep to the subject matter that old William was obsessed with).

All the best,
Miss Moss

## When Kiffo Died

Some things are best forgotten, Mother said:
When spinning days are steeped in pain enough,
Why resurrect what's buried in the head?
But if we *can't* forget . . . that's when it's tough,
When images revolve against our will
And in our dreams press heavy on the eyes—
A red-haired boy, a car, a bike, a spill
Of earth and sky, a crumpled form that lies
Beside a road. The imprints of these things
Are stamped upon my mind. I see again
His hair, his freckled face and memory brings
The dead to life, refreshes like the rain.
    When Kiffo died I knew I'd lost a friend.
    I did not know the void would never end.

# Chapter 13

## Just your average date, part two

Jason was drop-dead gorgeous. He was wearing dark chinos and a collarless shirt. My head broke into a sweat as soon as I saw him. He smiled and I worried that a thin sheen of perspiration would slide from under my hat and baste my face, like those portable water features.

If Jason noticed anything about my head, he didn't say anything. The hat I was wearing was floppy all right, but close examination would reveal an absence of tresses flowing down my back. I tried to keep facing him. He'd find out soon enough, but I wanted to be in control of the timing.

We picked up tickets. He paid, thank God, and I didn't protest too much. Independent creature though I am, the fact that my checking account held one dollar and twenty-four cents militated against chipping in. Jason suggested we have a drink before the film started, as we had forty-five minutes to kill, and I was happy with that. For one thing I wanted to get the revelation over with as quickly as possible. If he hated my scalp, there was still time to call the date off. I didn't want to be sitting next to someone in the cinema and know he would sooner have his toenails ripped out with red-hot pliers than be seen there by any of his friends.

It was getting to make-or-break time.

We sat down outside Giorgio's, a little Italian coffee shop on the outskirts of the mall, and ordered two hot chocolates. Jason wanted to sit outside to smoke and I didn't object. If you were going to do a grand unveiling, then it was fitting to do so in front of the entire city. Maybe there'd be speeches and a ribbon-cutting.

"Love the hat," said Jason. God, his eyes were gorgeous.

"Thanks," I said. I took it off.

There were gasps all around. Traffic screeched to a halt. Passersby stopped and stared. The only sound was of jaws hitting concrete and the smash of coffee cups as twenty waiters dropped their bundles. A caged parrot in the shop window fell off its perch.

Actually, I'm not sure any of that happened. It might have been my imagination. You'll have to use your judgment.

Certainly there was a lull in the conversation. Jason froze, the cup against his lips, a thin smear of hot chocolate giving him an artificial mustache. Actually, it looked cute. Finally he put the cup back on its saucer and wiped his top lip.

"You're bald," he said.

"There's not much that gets past you," I replied. "What gave you the first clue?"

Jason: It suits you. (*You look like a bouncer.*)

Calma: Do you really think so?

Jason: Sure. It's distinctive. It's different. (*It's shit.*)

Calma: I like to be individual.

Jason: Did you get it done for Shave for a Cure? (*Or am I dealing with someone who's two sandwiches short of a picnic?*)

Calma: Yes. A spur-of-the-moment thing. I thought, "Hell, why not?" It's for a good cause.

Jason: Nice one. (*I'll create a diversion and make a run for it. With luck I'll be able to shake her off after a couple of miles.*)

Calma: I thought you might hate it.

Jason: Of course not. (*Of course I do, you bald drongo.*) It was just a shock, that's all. (*To find I was dating an extra from* Lord of the Rings.) Actually it accentuates your features. (*Who was that bald guy in* The Addams Family?)

Calma: Is that good?

Jason: Absolutely. (*Not.*)

You see, part of the problem is that when someone is saying all the right things, you don't know if they are saying all the right things because they feel they need to say all the right things or whether they are saying all the right things because those are the things they want to say.

Do you see what I'm trying to say? It's a tricky one.

And then I got the answer. Jason laughed. He tried not to. In fact, he was taking a sip of his chocolate and he ended up inhaling part of it. So he's spluttering with laughter and asphyxiation, and that started me off. Some people at adjoining tables laughed as well. It was infectious. And I knew it wasn't malicious laughter. You can tell these things. Jason was laughing because he was happy to be there. So was I.

It took a few minutes to recover. Just when we thought we had it under control, we'd start again. Eventually, though, we got a grip.

"So you don't feel like you're on a date with Uncle Fester, then?" I said.

"Hey, one of my favorite characters. Honest, it looks wicked. David Beckham in his shaved phase."

"And that's a compliment, is it?"

"They don't come much higher."

It was such a relief. I mean, I had done that rationalization business about shallow people judging on superficial appearances, but it would have hurt if he'd left me there at a coffee shop, all bald, dressed up, and nowhere to go. And if I was honest, I had to look at it from another perspective. What if Jason had turned up radically different from what I had been expecting? What if he'd had a huge boil covering part of his face? Would I have laughed it off, or would I have visited the ladies', climbed through a back window, and slipped off into the night?

I think I know the answer, but you can't tell for sure unless it happens.

We talked and he was really good company. I like the British sense of humor and he had it in spades. All the magazines I've ever read said a sense of humor is the biggest turn-on for women. I think that's true. It's certainly true when you've got a guy with a sense of humor *and* the kind of looks that turn your legs to jelly.

The start time of the film was approaching and I got up. Jason put a hand on my arm.

"Can you sit down a moment and tilt your face toward the tablecloth?" he said.

"Why?"

"There isn't a mirror around and I need to check my hair."

Bastard.

I really liked this guy.

The film was pretty good. It had pirates, which is always a positive sign, and the swashbuckling was awesome. There was scarcely one swash that didn't get a damn good buckle before the final credits. You can divide pirates into two categories, I decided. There was your heartthrob pirate with flashing teeth, bulging biceps, and full tights, and your unsightly pirate with missing limbs, decaying teeth, and speech impediments.

I tell you, if you were a pirate in those days and couldn't afford decent private medical insurance, you were in deep shit.

Anyway, like I said, the film was fun. It didn't stretch the mental faculties, but the special effects were good and few people of my acquaintance judge the quality of films by any other criterion. I saw Vanessa. She came over during the previews and asked if I'd put my hat on, since I was dazzling row H. Everyone's a comedian these days. I introduced her to Jason in a whisper and asked if she'd like to meet up afterward, but she said no. She was going straight to her dad's place. I have to confess I wasn't disappointed.

When the film finished, Jason asked if I'd like to go to a club or something. I didn't. For one thing, the lightness in my purse was getting to me and I felt uncomfortable about Jason paying for everything. Anyway, I wasn't in the mood for flashing lights and loud music. I had visions of standing in the middle of the dance floor, my head acting like one of those suspended disco balls. To be honest, I just wanted something quiet, so I suggested a walk.

We strolled along the banks of the river that runs through the center of town. Plenty of people were out. It was Friday night, after all, and the riverside is the hub of social life in my city. The weather was mild. The river glittered under streetlights and a nearly full moon shimmered on its surface. Knots of people sat looking out over the city or laughing and chatting in cafés. We didn't say much. At one stage Jason held my hand.

We sat on a bench overlooking the water, his knee pressing against my leg. I suddenly felt nervous. Jason squeezed my hand and turned toward me.

"Calma?" he said, looking intently into my eyes.

"Yes, Jason?" I whispered, desperately trying to keep blood from flooding my face. I'd read somewhere that Indian mystics can control metabolism by sheer willpower. If someone can slow their heartbeat to three beats a minute, then surely I could stop a blush in its tracks. There was silence for ten loud heartbeats: about four seconds. I lifted my face to his and closed my eyes.

"Who do you think is going to win the Premiership?"

I scrunched my eyes tighter, as if this was an agonizing question I had been pondering the entire evening. I puffed my cheeks out and blew through shuddering lips. Tricky, tricky question. I tried to drag up the name of the one soccer club I knew. Luckily, Jason continued, which gave me more time to dredge the murky depths of memory.

"I mean, you did say you wanted to continue the conversation about soccer."

I nodded violently.

"Sure. It's just . . . well, there's a number of teams that could win. . . ."

"But on current form?"

"Oh. On current form. Well, I'd have to say . . . and I'm sticking my neck out here, taking a bit of a punt, don't quote me . . . I'd have to say . . . Liverpool." The name popped into my mind at the last moment and I grabbed hold of it gratefully.

"But they're twenty points behind the leaders."

"I know, but there's still time."

"With six games to go, you reckon they'll overtake Crewe Alexandra?"

"On current form, yes, I do!" *Be confident, Calma, and keep it simple.*

"What, even though the maximum points available are eighteen and they're twenty points behind Arsenal and Crewe Alexandra aren't even in the Premiership?"

There was silence for a couple of seconds. "Stranger things have happened," I said, on the principle that I didn't have anything left to lose.

He laughed and his eyes got these terrific crinkles around them.

"Well, no. They haven't, actually."

"When did you know?" I said.

"That you didn't know your midfield from your flat back four? Right from the start. I was cracking on about stuff and you were like a rabbit caught in the headlights."

"Does it matter? That I lied to you about it? I mean, I'm interested in learning and everything. If you want, you could teach me—"

He kissed me on the lips and my stomach, previously at a cruising altitude of thirty thousand feet, plunged to a whisker above ground level. His mouth was warm and he tasted faintly of cigarette smoke and popcorn. My first kiss! (If we forget Kyle Colby in Year 5, who did it for a bet and wouldn't talk to me afterward.) There, on the bench, by the river. It was soft, and plucked at something just beneath my rib cage. I felt dizzy.

"Does it seem like it matters?" he said when we broke off.

In the mellow afterglow I told him the real story behind my hairdo. It wasn't something I had anticipated revealing, but it seemed right to get all the little deceptions off my chest. I thought he would see the funny side of it and he did. We spent so much time laughing.

It was a brilliant date. I mean, I know there are some of you out there who'd consider a date a complete failure without popping a pill, experimenting with some of the trickier maneuvers in the *Kama Sutra*, getting shit-faced on cask wine, and ending up marinating in your own vomit on the floor of the ladies' room at the local nightclub.

Well, call me old-fashioned, but I couldn't imagine anything nicer than walking along the riverbank, watching the lights of the city, hand in hand with Jason. Frangipani petals were blowing in the balmy evening breeze. Cupid had my heart in his sights at point-blank range and was in the process of loosing the arrow when I saw her again.

The Fridge.

She was walking slowly on the path directly opposite where we were standing. On the other side of the river. Like me, she was giving all the signs of being insufferably content, bathed in her own emotional glow, gazing into the night sky as if the world had been born afresh. Like me, she was hand in hand with a guy.

I couldn't see who it was. She was on the outside and obscuring my vision so I only got tantalizing glimpses. Other people were strolling by and that didn't help either. I grabbed Jason's hand hard and looked for the nearest bridge over the river.

"Come on," I said, and pulled him back from where we had come.

Jason may have been puzzled, but to be fair to him, he was game. Maybe it was all that interest in soccer, but he didn't seem averse to a late-night sprint with a bald chick for no apparent purpose. Then again, I didn't give him much option. I held onto his hand with a viselike grip and towed him over the bridge. The Fridge had been some distance from us when I started and I wasn't confident we'd catch up, even though she had been wandering along like a drugged wombat.

Sure enough, by the time we made it over the bridge, the crowds had swallowed her and her mysterious companion. I scanned faces and Jason panted for breath. Clearly his interest in sports didn't extend to actually doing any, unless there was an Olympic category in marathon smoking.

"I'm knackered," he said, gulping for air. "I hate to sound like a total wally, but was there any point to that?"

"I thought I saw someone."

I didn't feel like telling him more. It was our first date, after all. Anyway, what was there to tell? I smiled at him and tried to recapture the romantic moment we had enjoyed prior to spotting the Fridge. But my smile felt artificial and I knew the evening was effectively over.

I felt upset by the Fridge's behavior. I suppose it was something as simple as jealousy. She had a private life, something from which I was being deliberately excluded, as if she didn't even trust me to be pleased for her. Why would she do that? There was only one answer. Because I *wouldn't* be pleased for her. Not if the guy was my dad. I didn't see him properly, true. It's not something that would stand up in a court of law, granted. But logic told me it had to be him. The more I thought about it, the more I felt sad. Worthless. I suddenly wanted to go home.

I turned to explain this to Jason and my eye was caught by

a figure sitting on a bench across the river. The very bench that had been the scene of my first kiss.

Vanessa was sitting by herself, head bowed almost to her knees. Her overnight bag sat forlornly on the ground between her feet. There was something so unutterably pathetic and depressed about her posture that I knew she was crying. I couldn't actually see it at that distance, but I knew it as surely as if I had been sitting next to her. I was tempted to make another run for it, but didn't think Jason's lungs would stand another pounding. What was it with this evening? I always seemed to be in the wrong place.

Anyway, before I could even think about crossing that bloody bridge again, Vanessa got to her feet. She moved slowly, as if a weight was pressing on her and the effort of raising it was painful. She stood and wiped her eyes briefly with a sleeve. Then she picked up her bag and shuffled off along the river bank, away from me. I tell you, there was something in the way she moved that made tears prick behind my eyes. I had never seen anyone who seemed so steeped in unhappiness.

I stood for a while watching her slow progress, unaware of Jason standing next to me examining my face.

"What's the score, Calma?" he said eventually.

I snapped myself out of it. I became aware suddenly that I was rigid with tension and I was gripping Jason's hand so tightly my knuckles were white. It must have been unnerving for him. I forced another smile.

"Nothing," I said. "I want to go home now."

"Sure," he said. "I'll walk you."

And he did. On the doorstep he asked if I wanted to go out with him again. I did. I certainly did. And I told him that. But I was worried and distracted. Maybe, as a result, my tone of voice wasn't altogether convincing. His face was puzzled and closed as I shut the door. I was sorry about that, but only vaguely.

All I wanted to do was go to bed. It had been a very strange evening and I couldn't help but think it was a precursor to stranger evenings to come.

# Chapter 14

## Calma hits the trail

"Did you have fun last night?" asked the Fridge. "And why are you wearing a towel around your head?"

It was Saturday morning and I was picking at a round of toast. The Fridge was drinking coffee.

"Yeah, great," I replied, ignoring her second question. "How was work?"

"Oh, you know. Work is work. Nothing to write home about. Tell me about your evening."

Okay. There were two ways this could go. Let's call the first one *The Seriously Mature Daughter Tackles Her Mother Head-On About Issues Important to the Integrity of Their Relationship.* The plot would undoubtedly unfold like this:

> *Calma Harrison popped the last piece of toast into her mouth and gazed steadfastly at her mother. She had come to a decision. She was not going to allow their relationship to*

**113**

become tarnished by omissions, half-lies, and outright whoppers. The time had arrived for plain speaking.

"Mother," she said, "I saw you last night, in the company of a gentleman. Now, for some reason, possibly to protect me from potential feelings of jealousy and abandonment, you have kept this liaison quiet, even to the extent of fabricating alibis that you were in gainful employment during the time of these romantic trysts. I feel, Mother—and I have to be brutally frank here—betrayed by your lack of trust. I am no longer a child. If you have found a soul mate, even if it is someone I might consider to be less than the dust beneath your chariot wheels, then the very least I deserve is that you share your feelings with me."

Mrs. Harrison looked into her coffee cup and a tear slid down her cheek. She didn't speak for a moment, but when she did, her voice cracked with emotion.

"Oh, Calma," she said, "I have been foolish not to trust you. What you have said, albeit rather wordy, has hit the emotional and intellectual target. I am, indeed, involved in a romantic association and, furthermore, have made the serious miscalculation of indulging in duplicitous practices with regard to communicating such a state of affairs with the only fruit of my loins. I stand justly accused. But Calma"— and here she raised her eyes to meet her daughter's—"you must believe I was acting according to the dictates of my conscience."

"I freely acknowledge this, Mother," said Calma, "though, incidentally, I feel a touch aggrieved at your accusation of

*overblown linguistic flourishes, which, coming from you, is a*
*little akin to receiving a sermon on pacifism from al-Qaeda.*
*But enough of that; the identity of your new* amour?"

   *"His name is Jerome. He is the chairman of a large multi-*
*national telecommunications company and owns apartments*
*in Sydney, Paris, London, and New York, not to mention a*
*luxury oceangoing yacht and a medium-sized island in the*
*Whitsundays. He has proposed and I have accepted. . . ."*

Let's call the next *The Seriously Pissed-Off Daughter Sucks her Thumb and Throws a Tantrum.*

   "Tell me about your evening," said the Fridge.

   "It was good."

   "Is that it? 'Good'? This was your first date!"

   "Yeah."

   "Where did you go?"

   "Movies."

   "What film did you see?"

   "Dunno."

   "You don't know? How can you have forgotten already?"

   "Something with pirates."

   "Was it good?"

   "All right."

   "Come on, tell me. What was Jason like? How did you guys get on?"

   "All right."

   You get the picture. I wasn't in the mood. And before you start blaming me, put yourself in my position. Here's my mother trying to get me to dish on *my* date, yet she couldn't bring herself to acknowledge that *she'd* been on one herself. Maybe you're a saint, but I'm certainly not. I was going to tell her bugger all. I kept the towel wrapped tightly. Everyone else might know about my shaved head, but I wasn't going to give her the satisfaction, even of common knowledge. She didn't deserve it.

Okay, I was angry. And confused. And worried. Not just about the Fridge but about Vanessa as well. I hadn't slept much. The image of a girl hunched on a bench had come between me and sleep. She seemed so lonely, so defeated. I regretted not running after her the previous night, but there was no point in berating myself with things that couldn't be changed. I needed to talk to her but had no idea where her father lived. I wasn't even sure Aldrick was his last name. In fact, the more I thought about it, the more convinced I became that Nessa and her mother had reverted to a previous name after the divorce. It was only a niggling half-memory—like I said before, I couldn't remember Vanessa talking about her father— but it felt right.

The Fridge tried to draw me out, but I was like a clam with additional superglue. Then she changed tack. I shouldn't have been surprised.

"Calma," she said, "don't you think it'd be a good idea to talk to your dad? He told me he'd tried, but you wouldn't have anything to do with him. Couldn't you give him a chance? Just listen to what he has to say?"

I didn't bother replying and eventually she gave up and disappeared somewhere in the car. I didn't ask where. Why bother, when you have no idea if the answer you're going to get has even a passing acquaintance with the truth? Anyway, she left, all tight-lipped and seething with resentment at my lack of communication. She's got a bloody nerve, I'll give her that. And my dad. When was he going to stop screwing up my life?

As soon as she was out the door, I was on the phone. Mrs. Aldrick answered after a few rings.

"Hi, Mrs. Aldrick," I said. "It's Calma. I'm sorry to bother you, but I need to get in touch with Vanessa and I don't have her father's number. I wondered if you could let me have it."

There was a gasp at the end of the line, as if I'd told her I was holding her daughter ransom and unless she dropped three million dollars in a trash bin at the local mall, I'd be mailing amputated extremities to her at regular intervals.

"I'm sorry, Calma," she said eventually, "but I can't give out her father's number. He's very strict about that."

"Oh, come on, Mrs. Aldrick," I said with a hint of exasperation. "It's me. Her best friend. I mean, I'm not going to post it on the Internet or anything. And I do need to talk to her."

"I'm sorry, Calma. His number is unlisted for a reason."

I could tell by her tone of voice that I was up against an immovable object. I had to think laterally.

"Well, how about you call her and tell her to contact me? That would be okay, wouldn't it?"

There was silence at the other end of the phone. I could

almost hear the cogs whirring. I mean, it was a perfectly reasonable request. No one could object to it. So why was her silence swollen with reluctance?

"I can't do that, Calma. This is Vanessa's time with her father and I will not intrude on it." There was triumph in her voice, as if she'd found a foolproof defense against checkmate. The trouble was, the defense *did* seem solid. I hate losing. It makes me mad. And then I want to get even.

"Okay, Mrs. Aldrick. Vanessa's back . . . when? On Sunday evening?"

"Yes. Quite late, usually."

"Can you get her to call me as soon as she gets back? Doesn't matter how late."

"I'll tell her, but you might have to wait until school on Monday. She normally just wants to drop straight into bed."

What was it with this woman? Talk about putting obstacles in the way. I hung up, my politeness stretched to breaking point, and sat in the garden for a while, thinking. As far as Vanessa was concerned, I couldn't see a way around the problem. Her dad must live downtown—I couldn't imagine Vanessa getting a bus at that time of the evening, so it was a reasonable assumption she was walking to his place immediately after her tearful spell on the bench. I suppose I could have wandered around in the hope of spotting her, but the chances were remote, to say the least. I reluctantly came to the conclusion that I would have to wait until school on Monday.

That left the Fridge. The mystery surrounding her might have been solved by the direct approach, but my pride wouldn't allow it. If she was going to be secretive, I could be even more secretive. I'd find out, in my own way, whom she was seeing. If it was my father, then I'd head for the Galapagos Islands by myself. But if it was a new boyfriend, I'd humiliate her with prior knowledge. I had visions of a conversation in which I'd say, *Oh, a boyfriend, Mum. You mean that Mr. Jones you've been seeing for the last month and a half? Tall guy, works in insurance in the city, lives in an apartment on Mitchell Street, divorced, forty-two, has a birthmark shaped like a sperm whale on his left buttock? Oh, I've known about him for ages. . . .*

Yes. I was going to solve this enigma.

The trouble was, I didn't have a clue how.

The solution presented itself when the Fridge reappeared, carrying bags of groceries. Call me a genius if you must, but the idea flashed fully formed into my mind. I needed some information first, though, so I bustled through to the front of the house and helped the Fridge get more bags from the trunk. She was surprised by this spontaneous act of helpfulness. I tried a cheery smile, exuding the air of someone now entirely at peace with the world, instead of the premenstrual harridan I'd been impersonating before.

"Do you want me to put these away, Mum?" I said.

"Thanks," she replied.

"Are you going in to work today?" I shoved packets of pasta into the kitchen cupboard and attempted to sound nonchalant.

"Yes. Four o'clock. Why?"

"Oh, I just wondered if you could give me a lift, that's all."

"But you start work at five yourself, don't you?"

Bugger. I'd forgotten about that. The last thing I felt like was going into Crazi-Cheep, but I didn't have much choice. You can't throw a sickie when you've only worked a week. And anyway, there were compensations. Like it was also Jason's shift. And I was going to get paid. About four dollars and fifty cents, probably, but it was better than nothing. I did some quick calculations. Even though I would only have an hour between her shift and mine, I thought it might be enough time to make a start, at least. I'd give it a go.

"Oh, yeah," I said. "I'd forgotten. Good thing you reminded me."

The Fridge stopped putting a carton of milk in her namesake and gave me a long, searching look.

"Are you okay, Calma?" she said. "You seem . . . I don't know. Distracted. And you have a bath towel welded to the top of your head, for no apparent reason. There isn't anything you'd like to tell me, is there?"

"Like a secret I'm keeping from you?"

She looked at me even more funnily then.

"Yeah. I suppose so."

I put on a broader smile.

"Would I keep secrets from you, Mum?" I said sweetly. And that seemed to end the conversation.

I'd given the Fridge every chance to come clean, but she'd spurned the opportunity. If there was any part of me feeling bad about the plan I had formulated, it disappeared at that moment. Actually, I don't think there was any part, so it was a little academic. I thrust a bag of split peas into a dark corner of the cupboard, where the Fridge was unlikely to ever spot it, and went to my room. I told the Fridge I needed to study math, but it was just a cunning subterfuge.

What I really wanted to do was perfect my disguise.

Now, how do you go about changing your appearance so that not even your mother would recognize you? I suppose my barren dome gave me a head start, if you'll forgive the pun, but I was uneasy about going out without some kind of covering. Sure, the Fridge would be unlikely to associate a skinhead with her own daughter, but it was a style that attracted exactly the attention I wanted to avoid. So I fished the blond wig from her wardrobe and stashed it under my bed.

I then turned to my own wardrobe. There were articles of clothing in there that hadn't seen daylight in years. The Fridge used to make a habit of searching through secondhand shops for the most appalling fashion disasters and then presenting them to me triumphantly, as if I was going to be thrilled at receiving stuff other people had thrown out for quite obvious reasons.

Still, it's a favorite maxim of mine that you never know when something might come in handy. I pulled out a short red skirt that would have come to my knees when I was thirteen but which now would be useful only as a broad belt. I tried it on and it fitted around the waist beautifully but exposed so much of my legs I wouldn't dare bend over in public. I also found a glittery silver top. A pair of high-heeled black shoes, which I dusted off with another top, completed the outfit. I put on the blond wig and surveyed myself in the mirror.

It was then I discovered what the Fridge had been attempting to achieve when she bought all this junk. She'd wanted me to be a child prostitute. It was the only explanation. It was strangely empowering. In this getup I could do anything I liked and wouldn't feel any responsibility. You know, a kind of Jekyll and Hyde thing.

*During the day, she is meek, mild Calma Harrison, librarian to the elderly and infirm, but at night she is transformed into . . . Super Slut!*

I glanced at my watch. There was still time for the final touch to my disguise: makeup. I didn't hold back there either, I can tell you. I put it on with a trowel, and my lack of expertise proved a distinct advantage. Bright, glossy lips and enough black mascara to make my eye sockets seem as if they were suffering a lunar eclipse. I had the face of a nymphomaniac panda.

I stuffed a change of clothes into a plastic shopping bag and glanced out my bedroom window. The car was still in the driveway, but my watch told me the Fridge would be making tracks very soon. I tiptoed out of my room and listened at the top of the stairs. The toilet in the bathroom flushed and I knew the coast was temporarily clear. I clattered down to the hallway, nearly breaking my ankles in the high heels, and opened the front door. Fortunately, the street was deserted and as far as I could tell there were no curtains twitching across the road.

I yelled up the stairs to the Fridge.

"I'm off now, Mum. Catch you later."

There was a muffled reply, but I closed the front door and scuttled round to the side of the car. Making sure the car body was between me and any windows in the house, I carefully opened the rear door and bundled myself into the well behind the driver's seat.

Now, you need to understand something about the family vehicle. I believe it is the custom in some households to regularly polish and wax the exterior, vacuum the interior, buff the rearview mirror and generally maintain an atmosphere of cleanliness and hygiene. The Fridge treats the car like a giant trash barrel. There are potato chip packets, battered cups from McDonald's, copies of the local newspaper with screaming headlines like "Titanic 0, Iceberg 1," and other assorted detritus. You could hide an elephant seal in the back of the car and be confident the Fridge would never notice.

I tucked myself down and pulled an old curtain over my head. Don't ask me what it was doing there, all right?

Fortunately, I didn't have to wait long. I heard the Fridge slam the front door and felt the car dip as she got behind the wheel. The engine spluttered into life and the car lurched into reverse. We were on our way. I hoped it wasn't going to be a long trip and not just because I only had an hour to get there, trail the Fridge, and make it back to Crazi-Cheep in time for my shift. You see, the car doesn't have AC, unless you count a faulty front window liable to slip down, and it was a hot day.

I risked lifting the curtain a little, just to get some air. It didn't help much. It was still like being in the waiting room for Hades, but at least I could see. In fact, I discovered a plastic doll I had lost when I was five years old.

I'd always liked that doll.

Twenty minutes later, the car came to a halt and the engine cut out. I was relieved, I can tell you. The Fridge gathered her stuff from the passenger seat. Then the car door slammed and the key turned in the lock. This was the tricky part. How long should I wait before I got out of the car? If it was too soon, the Fridge would spot me, but if I left it too long, then she might have disappeared and the whole exercise would have been futile. Judgment was vital.

I waited until the clack of her shoes faded and then counted slowly to ten. I slowly pushed open the rear door and slipped into a pool of sunshine. Snapping the lock down, I pushed against the door until I could feel the mechanism engage. Only then did I search for the Fridge.

I was in the parking lot of the casino. Of course. Just my luck. The one time the Fridge actually goes to work was bound to be the day I followed her. I looked toward the entrance of the casino, about two hundred yards away, but could see no sign of her. She couldn't possibly have walked that distance in the time.

I couldn't believe it. Had the earth swallowed her?

I pivoted around, a dangerous maneuver in high-heeled shoes, and just as I was about to despair completely, I spotted her. She was standing in the middle of the parking lot, talking to a man. He was holding my mother by the arm, in a curiously intimate way, just by the elbow. She was looking up into his face and smiling. It *had* to be the same man I'd seen last night. I couldn't imagine the Fridge made a habit of romantic assignations with different people. Even though I couldn't get a good view because he had his back to me, it cleared up one concern. It wasn't my dad. This guy had hair. Lots of it, mostly gray. But who was he? I started to walk toward them and that's when the first disaster happened.

The man dropped my mother's arm and opened a car door for her. She dipped her head and got in. He walked around to the driver's side and got behind the wheel, and there was a throaty roar from a powerful engine. They were driving off! I tried to walk faster. I would have broken into a run, but the high heels were a danger to life and limb. How do women wear them and steer clear of hospital emergency rooms? I kept tottering to the side and my ankles bowed alarmingly. My call-girl persona now had the additional refinement of apparent inebriation. I watched helplessly as the car, a long, sleek beast, swept past. The Fridge and the driver were gazing into each other's eyes, so they didn't notice me. I doubt if they would have noticed if Elvis had materialized on the hood.

The car disappeared down the casino's driveway and headed away from town, fading into a dim twinkle of brake lights. I hadn't even had the presence of mind to get the license plate.

Sweaty, irritated, and feeling completely dispirited, I staggered into the casino. I needed the ladies' room. There was a bloke standing guard at the entrance, all done up in formal gear, but looking like a hulking slab of muscle. You know the kind. Squashed nose, perpetual stubble, and a brain the size of a pea. He leered as I approached, his piggy eyes glued to my silvered, sparkling bust.

"Not a bloody word, mate," I said to him, "or you'll find the business end of these stilettos giving you a rectal exploration."

I left him struggling to find a response and crashed open the door of the ladies' toilet. Haunted, black-rimmed eyes stared back at me from the mirror. I was exhausted. And it was then, when I was at my lowest, that the second disaster broke into my consciousness.

I had left the bag with my change of clothes in the car.

The locked car.

And if that wasn't bad enough, my purse and house keys were in it as well. I contemplated the half-hour walk back to Crazi-Cheep, in high heels, in the blazing sun, dressed like a hooker, and I started to cry.

It did absolutely nothing for the mascara.

# Chapter 15

## From harlot to heroine

If it's all the same to you, I'll let the details of my long walk to work remain in oblivion. Maybe deep hypnosis could resurrect the grisly experience, but some things are best left buried.

I'll tell you one thing, though. It was not a happy, carefree Calma Harrison who finally staggered through the doors of Crazi-Cheep on Saturday afternoon. It was a Calma Harrison in the mood for violent confrontation with any pensioner who glanced at her sideways. I burst through the automatic doors looking like Sexually Deviant Barbie. Mothers grasped small children to their bosoms as I clicked toward the staff changing rooms. I couldn't see Jason. That was the only bright spot in an otherwise bleak situation.

At least I had the opportunity to clean myself up. Typically, the store only provided cheap Crazi Brand soap for its employees, but it did the trick. The mascara was stubborn, though. By the time I'd finished scrubbing my eyes with gritty soap, the redness around my face made it seem like I had been sobbing hysterically for a large portion of the millennium. For once I was grateful for the outsized uniform. I stripped down to my underwear and unless a freak tornado careered down aisle twelve and lifted up my uniform, I would remain decent. The wig had to go, as did the high heels. Those things were spawned from a mind of pure evil.

I marched from the changing room straight to House-wares, where I picked up a multicolored dish towel and folded it into a bandanna. With my red eyes and a tea towel on my head, I resembled the late Yasser Arafat, but I didn't give a stuff. From there, I went to the section that had flip-flops. My trans-formation from *Penthouse* Pet to middle-aged housewife com-plete, I fronted up to Candy at customer service to inquire about my duties for the evening.

I was hoping she would say something about my appear-ance. I was in that kind of mood—the sort where if someone says, "Good evening," you're liable to give them a stiff-fingered poke in the throat. But she just assigned me to shelf stacking again.

That didn't improve my mood either. I wanted to say, *Oh, I was good enough for the registers when you were desperate, but now the brain-dead zombies you call your staff have returned, I'm back to the chorus line, is that it?* I didn't, though. It was just another small flame under my simmering anger.

I plunged through the plastic curtains out the back and loaded up a cart with sundry items apparently in short supply on the shelves. I grunted at one of the men when he smiled and said *hello*. Provocative bastard!

I was slamming cans of something onto a shelf and cursing softly under my breath when there was a tap on my shoulder. I resisted the urge to slam a can backwards into a rheumatic ankle and got wearily to my feet.

It was my father. Of course it was. How could it be anyone else? Maybe the Grim Reaper, but frankly that would have been preferable. I narrowed my reddened eyes and tried to get his head to explode through sheer force of will. I saw a film where that happened once.

"Calma," he said. "You look different."

"Unfortunately," I said, "you look exactly the same. Please rearrange these words into a well-known phrase or saying: *off, piss.*"

"Please," he said. "I'll leave you alone. But first there's something I need to tell you. Come on, Calma. Please."

"You haven't a clue, have you?" I replied, the steel in my voice getting harder and sharper by the moment. "Not the vaguest idea of what you've done to Mum and me. Otherwise you wouldn't be here. Well, matey, if you want to know the cold, hard facts of the matter, you lost your chance to talk to me when you walked out five years ago. I remember. I remember sitting on the stairs, listening to you shouting. And you stormed past me as if I wasn't there and the next thing you were gone. Talking wasn't of any significance then, was it? Why should I believe anything's changed?"

"Calma," he said, "I *have* tried to talk to you. I have. But you . . . Listen, isn't it possible you might have lost perspective on this?"

"No, but it's certain you've lost my interest," I replied. "Please go. Stop haunting this store like some sad ghost father of Christmas past. Stop following me. Just stop everything. Breathing included. Keep out of my life!"

His eyes widened. I had difficulty myself believing what I'd said, but this was not the best time to engage me in even casual conversation, let alone a heart-to-heart with someone I wouldn't pee on if he was on fire.

"But Calma, I'm your father. You might not like it, but that doesn't change the fact we have a bond. A blood tie. And it isn't going to go away."

"Look," I said, "get fifty cents and call someone who gives a shit about your clichés. I have to work."

I turned back to slam more cans into empty spaces. Ironic, really, since empty spaces seemed to be all I was composed of at that moment. When I looked up, he had gone.

For a brief moment, I couldn't be sure if what I felt was relief or regret. But I readjusted my towel and turned my attention to the pressing matter of button mushrooms in brine. Life, as I knew only too well, had to go on.

My mood did not improve when I took my break. Jason was smoking in his usual spot round the corner, and at first he didn't see me. He didn't see me because he was busy talking to a blond girl who was giggling in a moronic fashion. She had big blue eyes, a wide mouth, and flawless teeth. I couldn't decide which of these features to punch first. She kept brushing back her hair whenever he said anything. Now, if you're male, you'll probably find this an entirely innocent mannerism. If you're female, however, you'll understand it's akin to shouting from the rooftops, *Come on, big boy. Let's get it on.* I hated her. I hated Jason.

Apparently he didn't understand this because when he saw me he gave me a big smile and came over to where I was slouched in abject depression against a wall.

"Hey, Calma. How's it goin'?"

"Who's your friend?" I replied in a tone of voice that could strip paint. Jason glanced back at the blond bimbo, who was fluttering her eyelashes and practicing her hair smoothing.

"Her?" he said, somewhat redundantly, since we were the only ones out there. "She's the new girl. We were just chatting."

"Happy days," I said. "It's not often chatting can produce that kind of effect on the female of the species."

"What are you on about?" he said, sounding genuinely puzzled.

"Oh, come off it, Jason," I said. "It was like watching the Discovery Channel. A few more minutes and she would have adopted a mating posture. The air's thick with pheromones. Or it could be the cheap perfume she's wearing. What is that, Canal Number 5?"

Jason smiled, which was entirely the wrong approach to take.

"Are you jealous, Calma?"

"Jealous?" I said. "Oh, please. You flatter yourself, my friend."

His smile broadened and the twisting sensation in my gut grew accordingly.

"You are," he stated.

I spluttered something incoherent as an encore and stormed back into the store.

I couldn't remember when I'd had a better day.

I decided to lose myself in my work. I careered around the store like that Tasmanian devil in the cartoon, all whirling shapes and blurs. Shelves were stacked in such a way that if you were an innocent bystander you'd swear time-lapse photography was going on. There is a theory, often espoused by the mindlessly optimistic, that physical work is a perfect antidote to pressing personal problems.

It's a crap theory. Maybe because the work *was* mindless and purely physical, I found myself focusing more and more on the problems besetting me. I was still no nearer a solution to the Fridge puzzle, Vanessa was off somewhere and miserable for reasons still unclear, and my boyfriend was oozing pure charm at a brain-dead blonde. At least she *had* hair she could fondle provocatively. I just had an expanse of stubbly scalp. So it was all I could do to remain reasonably polite when some guy tapped me on the shoulder to ask directions.

He was a runt, with the complexion of an avocado. A

small wisp of hair on his top lip gave him the look of someone desperately trying to appear older than he was. I guessed he couldn't be much older than me. He had spiked his hair with gel and looked like the kind of bloke who tied cans to the tails of dogs and thought the height of sophistication was farting during science lessons and shouting, "Who cut the cheese?" Don't get me wrong. I don't normally judge on appearances, but I was in a bad mood and prepared to make an exception in his case.

"Excuse me," he said. "Could you tell me where you keep stockings?"

"Stockings?" I said, aware I sounded irritated.

"Yeah, pantyhose. You know, the things women wear on their legs."

I was tempted, believe me. It was with a conscious effort of will that I stopped myself from telling him I was aware of the meaning of the word "stockings"; that if we were going to compare vocabularies, I'd outscore him by a factor of three thousand. But I didn't. Instead, I sighed and replied as reasonably as I could manage.

"Aisle fourteen, sir. Would you like me to show you? On the grounds I'd be surprised if you've mastered figures beyond ten?" Actually, I didn't say the last bit. He sounded relieved, though.

"Yeah. Would you?"

"This way, sir."

He followed me across the store and seemed nervous,

glancing all over the place as if expecting an ambush at any moment. He couldn't stop talking, either.

"They're for my girlfriend," he threw in, apropos of nothing.

"Really, sir?" I replied. "That is a relief. I'm not sure we've got any in your size."

"No. They're for my girlfriend. I'm buying them for her."

I could see that the conversation, having hit this dizzying height, was unlikely to soar beyond it.

"She's a very lucky woman," I lied outrageously. She was also going to be a very hot woman, I thought. I didn't know anyone who wore pantyhose. In the heat of the tropics, wearing stuff like that was a recipe for disaster. You might as well put up a neon sign saying, WELCOME. FUNGAL INFECTIONS, THIS WAY.

"Here we are, sir. What denier do you want?"

"Huh?"

"Thickness. Darkness. That sort of thing."

"Thick and dark."

*A little like yourself,* I thought.

"Well, these are the darkest we have. One size fits all."

"Great. Do you sell toys, too?"

"A present for yourself, sir?"

He shifted uncomfortably.

"Er, no. It's for my nephew."

"Well, we don't have a toy section as such, but near the checkouts you'll find our Bargain Buy area, where the products of billions of Chinese can be found in various shades of thin plastic and nothing is priced above two dollars."

**134**

"Thanks."

He scuttled off in pursuit of quality merchandise and I returned to aisle ten, where assorted tins of fruit awaited my expert ministrations. I was just wondering why anyone would ever purchase lychees in vinegar when a scream from the customer service desk echoed through the store. This was immediately followed by shouting and the crashing sound of displays falling. Given a choice between lychees and front-of-store drama, I think you'll agree there is little competition, so I went to see what the commotion was about.

It was the runt. He had the pantyhose on his head, and under other circumstances I would have applauded his sense of civic duty. This was a face best kept under wraps. However, he was also leaping around the checkouts, waving his arm about. His hand was hidden by something—it might have been a dish towel similar to the one wrapped around my head—and he was yelling at the top of his voice.

"I've got a gun, motherfuckers," he screamed. "Get down on the floor, all of youse. I want the money from the registers. No funny business, or I'll blow your fuckin' heads off."

I had time to admire the look on Candy's face. She had stopped chewing, for one thing, and panic was struggling to emerge. Then she slowly sank beneath her desk. It was a bizarre sight, as if she was standing on a trapdoor that was being cranked by degrees down into the bowels of the building. The other employees, Jason included, dived beneath their registers.

There was silence. The store was nearly deserted, which

explained why we had five people on the registers instead of one. The runt was capering about, brandishing his loaded towel.

Then he stopped and, even with stockings over his face, I could tell he was wearing a puzzled expression.

"The money!" he yelled. "Where's the fuckin' money?"

Candy's voice came faintly from beneath the desk.

"We can't stay on the floor *and* get the money from the registers. You'll have to make a choice."

I tell you, if brains were explosive, you could put Candy and the runt together and not have enough to blow your hat off. Or your towel. Or your pantyhose, come to that. The runt looked around as if for assistance and then strode over to checkout four. Jason's checkout.

"Okay," he yelled. "You! Get up and get the money out of your register. Stash it in this pillowcase. Then do the same for the other registers."

At least he had had the presence of mind to pick up a pillowcase from Housewares. Aisle thirteen, if memory served me correctly. Jason got up from the floor. His expression was sickly.

"I can't," he said.

"Just do it, motherfucker. I'm not kiddin'. I'll blow you away. I swear to God."

"I can't open the registers. You need the supervisor's key."

I don't know how long this little farce would have continued, but I was getting fed up. The way things were going, we'd be stuck in Crazi-Cheep for hours, until somebody got their act together. Plus I was pissed off.

I strode along the front of the aisles, stopping to pick up a stainless-steel frying pan (aisle twelve, $19.99—pretty good value, actually), and then headed toward checkout four, where the runt was twitching like a headless chicken. He saw me coming from afar.

"What the fuck do you think you're doin'?" he screamed. I was beginning to despair of this guy. Granted, he was in a pressure situation, but that's no reason not to vary the decibel count. I mean, after a while, being yelled at becomes passé. You need to mix it up. That's my theory, anyway.

"Get on the fuckin' floor," he continued.

I ignored him. I had it all worked out. The toy section? Yeah, right. He had picked up a water pistol or something. Let's apply a little logic here. What self-respecting robber would go to a store with a gun but without a disguise? No. He had picked up the pantyhose—I wished I'd recommended something lighter; they didn't really suit him—and then he had got a dish towel and a plastic piece of crap from the Bargain Buy section and that was it. All he needed for a heist. That and relying upon the staff being complete bozos. Well, he hadn't counted on Calma Harrison. I strode toward him and he lifted up the dish towel.

"Another step, motherfucker, and—"

"And what?" I said. "You'll dry all the dishes in the place? Listen, shitface, I've had a bad day. I am not the kind of person who has sexual relations with her own mother and I resent a sad, pathetic dropkick like you wasting my time."

And with that I smacked him on the head with the pan. It made a very satisfying clunk and he fell to the floor. I stood over him and saw his eyes rolling back in his head, even through the stockings.

There was silence. Then Jason appeared at my side.

"Jesus Christ, Calma," he said. "What have you done?"

"Mopped up a nasty spill," I said. "Part of my duties. Now I suggest you call the police while I go and finish off the canned fruit section."

I hadn't forgiven him for the blonde.

"But he was armed. You could have been killed!"

Jason's voice was cracking slightly and I noticed the decibel count was creeping up. If it continued, I'd smack him round the head with the pan as well. I was developing a taste for it. Instead, I put my hands on my hips, the pan sticking out behind like a small satellite dish, and turned my scorn upon him.

"Oh, please, Jason. What kind of a moron do you take me for? I mean, look. Stupid pantyhose on his head, mangy dish towel—aisle thirteen, four for five dollars—and a two-dollar plastic water pistol. He's not exactly Mr. Big from Sydney, trying to muscle in on the local organized-crime scene. He's just a pathetic bag of shit."

I kicked the runt's arm at that point, to punctuate my line of reasoning. The tea towel fell away and his arm flopped. A loud bang rang out and something ricocheted off the rent-a-carpet-cleaner display, taking out part of the skylight. There was a gentle shower of splintered glass and a smell of something burning.

I looked down at the runt's hand.

A black metal gun was gripped in his fingers, a thin wisp of smoke curling from the barrel.

There was only one thing to do. I fainted.

# Chapter 16

## Fifteen minutes of fame

## Leukemia Supporter Foils Supermarket Raid
### "She's a Heroine," Says Supervisor

A local resident foiled an attempted armed robbery at a supermarket late on Saturday night.

Calma Harrison, age sixteen, an employee at Crazi-Cheep supermarket, attacked the alleged thief with a stainless-steel frying pan, despite him being heavily armed and dangerous.

### Courageous

A police spokesperson described the intervention by Ms. Harrison as "courageous in the extreme. We certainly don't recommend members of the public taking direct action against armed robbers, but Ms. Harrison showed remarkable composure and bravery."

### Charity

Ignoring personal danger and armed only with a household utensil, Calma Harrison, who recently had her head shaved as part of the fundraising program in support of leukemia research, tackled the thief as he was in the process of emptying registers. "I just couldn't let him get away with it," she said. "Being an

Aussie battler, I knew I'd have to have a go. There were pensioners in the store and they could have been harmed. I didn't think about my personal safety. I just acted on instinct."

## Heroine

Candy Smith, the supervisor on duty, said, "Calma is a heroine. The guy was obviously crazy, but she tackled him straight on."

A local man is helping police with their inquiries.

In the interests of historical accuracy:

1. The newspaper article didn't come out until Monday.
2. I didn't say any of that stuff. I mean, would you really expect me to say something like, "I knew I'd have to have a go"? Does that sound like me? And as for "being an Aussie battler"—well, they could force me to wear stilettos and shred my epidermis with a paring knife, and I still couldn't bring myself to utter that phrase. They made all of it up.

Okay, I'll give you the shortened version. I woke up on the cold floor of the supermarket with Jason leaning over me. He looked concerned. I was too. It occurred to me I was wearing ratty underwear under my uniform and my fall might have rucked everything up, exposing things better hidden. As it turned out, it was all right.

The police made it there in quick time and I sat up just as they were cuffing the runt and bundling him, none too gently I might add, out of the premises. He hadn't recovered consciousness, and judging by the dent in the bottom of the frying pan, I suspected he would be out of it for some time.

Not even Candy could expect me to carry on working after that little episode. In fact, they closed the supermarket early, once the police had taken the names and addresses of everyone there. I was told they would be around to take a statement when I had recovered. To be honest, all of this went by in a blur. I do remember Jason walking me the short distance home. I didn't have the opportunity to tell him that if the Fridge was not home, I was locked out. Anyway, it was academic. The Fridge's car was in the driveway and there was a light on in the kitchen.

I don't know if she was more surprised by my bald head or the revelation that I had attacked a gunman with a frying pan. I was feeling queasy, if you want to know the truth, and took off to bed as soon as Jason left. The Fridge wanted to talk, but I was still pissed off at her and pleaded tiredness and ill health. I knew I would have plenty of explaining to do in the morning, but my bed called to me. I was asleep in minutes.

I dreamed of guns, mascara, men with long gray hair, and nonstick pans.

# Chapter 17

## Sunday, bloody Sunday

When I woke up in the morning, it took time for the previous day's events to come back to me. They had the texture of a dream. As the full significance of what I had done sunk in, my legs trembled. I was lying in bed, the sheets rippling all over the place. I was doing a horizontal performance of *Riverdance*. It took twenty minutes before I could think about swinging them over the bed and putting weight on them.

I had a shower and got dressed slowly. I wasn't looking forward to explaining everything to the Fridge and was happy to delay the inevitable. While I got ready I mentally prepared my own newspaper article.

# Bald Drongo in Supermarket Fiasco
## "What a Loser!" Says Supervisor

Police are considering charging local resident Calma Harrison, sixteen, with reckless endangerment of life after a bizarre series of events at Crazi-Cheep supermarket on Saturday night.

Harrison viciously attacked a customer with a frying pan, causing $19.99 worth of damage to the pan and $2,000 worth of damage to a skylight.

### Idiot

A police spokesperson described Ms. Harrison's actions as "reckless in the extreme. Frankly, we are fed up with members of the public having a go and thereby putting the lives of innocent people in jeopardy. If the idiot was my daughter, I'd slap her silly."

### Bald

Candy Smith, supervisor at Crazi-Cheep supermarket, said, "There will be a thorough investigation into the incident. Calma has been rude to customers before, but I didn't believe she'd attack one. I've worried about her since she started work, and when she turned up with a shaved head, I knew there was going to be trouble."

Calma Harrison was unavailable for comment last night. Police are monitoring all flights to the Galapagos Islands.

The Fridge was inhaling coffee when I made it down the stairs. She was dressed and appeared to be on the verge of going out, as normal. I stuck bread into the toaster and got a glass of milk as a delaying tactic.

"I like your head," said the Fridge as I was buttering my toast. "Very chic. Very shiny."

"For leukemia," I said. I wasn't in the mood for banter.

She cupped her hands around the coffee mug and blew into the steam. I sat opposite her at the kitchen table. Under most circumstances I can read the Fridge. She was thinking about whether she should be proud of me for what I had done last night or angry at me for putting myself in danger. I was curious which tack she'd take. The silence stretched and she glanced at her watch. My irritation grew.

"So," she said finally. "My daughter the heroine, huh?"

I kept quiet.

"Do you know," she continued, "I don't know whether to be proud of you or angry."

I kept quiet.

"Calma. Why don't we talk anymore?"

I wasn't prepared for that, but I recovered quickly.

"You've got to go, Mum, haven't you?" I said, dropping the piece of toast on my plate. "You keep checking your watch. You're going somewhere. Aren't you?"

She looked embarrassed.

"Well . . . yes," she said. "But I've got ten minutes. Maybe fifteen."

"You know," I said, pushing back my chair, "I've no idea why we don't talk anymore, Mum. It's a real mystery. Maybe we'll figure it out one day."

And I left. I went back to my bedroom, until I heard the front door close, the car start up, and the sound of the engine fade into the distance.

\* \* \*

I didn't know how to spend the day, mainly because there was nothing I wanted to buy with it. I wandered around the house. I thought about doing schoolwork but quickly discarded the idea. Then I thought about calling Jason, but I wasn't comfortable with that either. It wasn't so much the blonde. I decided I had overreacted, though I would rather die than admit it to Jason. I just thought I should wait until he called me.

In the end I turned on the TV and surfed channels. There was a soccer game on and I flicked past it, then thought better and skipped back. A scorecard in the top left of the screen told me it was Manchester United versus Liverpool.

Now, I know what you're thinking. *As soon as a guy comes on the scene, you watch soccer! Pretty soon you'll be dyeing your hair, if you had any, window-shopping for time-saving domestic appliances, and taking embroidery classes at night.* Yeah, well, I can understand this cynicism, but I want it placed on record that I'm the kind of person who is open to new experiences, who believes that minds are like sharks—if they stop moving, they die. Now, I'm not suggesting a soccer game will change your life. But I'd never seen one, and that's an omission. I had nothing better to do, after all.

Okay, smart-arse. I *had* remembered Jason supported Liverpool. *And* that I'd said I was prepared to learn about the game.

It's a strange business, soccer. At the final whistle I wasn't any wiser. As far as I could understand, to be a player you either had to have flowing locks, honed leg muscles, and a face with chiseled features or a stubbled pate and the kind of appearance that causes small children to wet themselves. There were plenty of these. At times they formed a line and put their hands over their private parts. This explained the general group ugliness. The ball, smacked at high velocity, must have rearranged a number of features that had previously been in tolerable condition. Their private parts, afforded protection, were undoubtedly in mint condition. It crossed my mind that some of them would have been better leaving their gonads alone and putting their hands across their faces.

I know I would have felt better.

The good-looking ones *were* good-looking, mind. They ran at full speed, kicking the ball toward the ugly ones, who would gently tap their finely honed legs, causing the hunky guys to scream in agony, roll over twenty times, and writhe on the ground. This would result in the lineup of willie-fondling ugly buggers previously mentioned. Getting injured at soccer is drastic, if short-lived. I mean, these guys react as if they're in the last stages of disembowelment, but within moments they are running around again, locks flowing and chiseled features intact.

The game involves getting the ball between the goalposts. Given that most players were trying to do this, it amazed me no one succeeded. In fact, the ball seemed to go everywhere *except* between the posts. Basic communication and elementary team-building skills should have enabled twenty-odd blokes to achieve this modest task. They were hopeless.

One part of the game I enjoyed enormously involved individual spitting contests. The players had a seemingly inexhaustible supply of phlegm. Every time the television camera was on them, they'd produce a huge slimy ball and blow it with considerable force into the ground. Sometimes they'd create divots. The more skilled were able to do this out their noses. They'd stick one finger against a nostril, closing it—presumably for maximum explosive potential—and send a tracer into the turf at the speed of sound. If they'd hit an opposing player in the leg, it would have had the same effect as a round from a .44 Magnum.

I enjoyed the game—in the same way as I'd enjoy watching an Italian opera. I didn't have a clue what was going on, but it was all very exciting. At least I'd have something to talk to Jason about. He could explain the snot hurling. Were there judges in the stands, awarding points for force, accuracy, and artistic interpretation? I'd ask him.

When the game was over, I tried Discovery, but it was a repeat so I turned the television off and attempted to read. I gave up after five minutes. I couldn't concentrate. I paced. I even thought about tidying my bedroom, but I hadn't yet reached the absolute pits of boredom, so I went into the garden and sat in a plastic chair.

I looked out over wilting palm trees and thought. My insides were a knot of anxiety. Or rather, a number of knots, all churning and mixing together. The Fridge, of course. And Vanessa. And Jason. My dad. But the more I thought, the more anxious I became and the more inextricable the mess of my personal relationships. I spent the rest of the day out there. I didn't even get anything to eat or drink. I didn't trust my stomach to keep it down.

Darkness fell abruptly, like it always does in the tropics, and I didn't budge. The stars freckled the sky and I watched. The more I stared, the more stars I saw—not directly, of course, but crowding the periphery of vision. If I concentrated on one spot, kept my gaze fixed, then stars appeared at the edge, one milky dot after another, until the sky became impossibly full. Apart from the black well, with its light dusting, in the center of my gaze. It occurred to me then that I spent too much time looking directly at things. Maybe I would see more if I watched less.

It seemed a profound realization at the time, but I had no idea how it could help.

I went to bed early. I unplugged the phone, took it with me, and plugged it into the phone jack in my bedroom. For some reason, I was incredibly tired. Maybe it was the emotional exertion of the night before. Maybe I was simply tired of thinking. But as I drifted off to sleep, I wondered why Jason hadn't called to see how I was. He'd been so concerned the night before, yet I had heard nothing from him all day. But if I'm honest, that wasn't the most important thing. What I really wanted was for Vanessa to call. I knew she would be home late from her dad's. If her mum gave her my message, and I wasn't convinced she would, then I wanted to be close to the phone when it rang.

It didn't. When the alarm went off at six-thirty, the first pale streaks of dawn were filtering through the curtains. They gave a sickly light and I didn't want to get up. The day offered no promise.

The phone, resolutely silent, lay on the floor beside my bed.

# Chapter 18

## The seal on the Fridge comes unstuck

*Dear Calma,*

I'm sorry. You're right. I can't complain about a lack of communication when I'm rarely around. Things are difficult at the moment. There's a lot going on. I'll tell you about it soon. Just give me time, please, and don't judge me too harshly. I love you, you know. I might not show it too often, but I do.

Keep Wednesday evening free, if you can (or you want). Birthday girl! I thought I'd take you and Jason for a meal. Invite Vanessa, if you like.

Love,

*Mum*

P.S. What do you want for a present?

*Dear Fridge,*

It's funny, isn't it? You want so badly to stay mad at someone, but as soon as they apologize, all those resolutions
evaporate. I would love to have a birthday meal with you.
Particularly at your expense. I'll ask Vanessa, and Jason if
the bastard ever deigns to call me.

There's only one thing I want from you for my birthday. More time. More conversation. More honesty. Sorry, I
guess that's three things. I know I sound corny, but it's true.

*Love,*

*Calma*

**From:** Miss Moss <moss.aj@lotis.edu.au>
**To:** Calma Harrison <harrison.c@lotis.edu.au>
**Subject:** Free verse

---

Calma,

As you know, free verse poetry follows no set rhythmical pattern. The writer uses her judgment to establish a pattern on the page. It is not an easy form to get right! You must be aware of the sound quality of individual words and how they can be put together to create music. And sense, of course.

Take a memory from childhood—any memory—and write a free verse poem that captures that memory and shows its effect upon you now.

Miss Moss

## The night my father left

The night my father left, he cried;
So Mother says—I don't recall.
The memory I possess predates that time—
A holiday, the three of us in snow,
Happy and powdered in laughter.
I lay on a bed of winter and watched
As, far above, a snowflake
(Individual as a poem in the oneness of its pattern)
Was minted, pressed from water and cold
In the stillness of the sky.
It crowded toward the gathering white below
Where, settling on the landscape of my face,
It fell in upon itself, shrank to a drop
I wiped away with my hand.

It is intensely sad,
The ease with which we brush aside
Something that can never be again,
With the semblance of a tear.

# Chapter 19

## Vanessa and the stars

Vanessa sat next to me in English, but we didn't get a chance to talk. Miss Moss set a close reading to do under timed conditions and it was a tricky little beggar. In fact, once I got into it, I forgot everything else. It's what athletes call "the zone"—an area of such concentration that a small incendiary device could be detonated next to you and you wouldn't blink. That's how I was with this piece of writing—totally absorbed by the ways the writer created atmosphere.

All right. You can smirk. Some people get fascinated with Justin Timberlake's facial hair, others with the relationship between sentence structure and characterization. Hey, everyone's different. So shoot me!

Anyway, the time flew and then it was math. Vanessa isn't in my math class, so I didn't catch up with her until lunch. I went down to our stamping ground by the canteen and there she was, gazing into the distance and nibbling another banana. I plopped myself beside her and followed her line of vision. As far as I could tell, she was staring at a trash bin on the edge of the oval. Even by the general standards of trash bins, this wasn't a particularly interesting one, but everyone has their personal "zone." We sat in companionable silence for a minute or two while I thought about the best way of broaching the subject of Friday night. Unfortunately, my thoughts were interrupted by Jamie Gallagher passing by and making an observation about my head, which was gloriously and unashamedly bare.

"Hey, Calma," he said. "Love the head. You know what would look good on it? A cue stick."

"Thanks, Jamie," I replied. "Do you know what would look good on your head? A pit bull terrier."

His eyes took on that pained glaze of concentration people get when they're searching for a clever response but can't find it. He scurried off, still thinking, and I turned to Vanessa.

"What did you think of the film on Friday?"

She turned her head so slowly I wondered if her neck mechanism was in need of service.

"Okay," she said finally, investing the judgment with no emotion whatsoever.

"Johnny Depp was hot, hey?"

"Okay, I guess."

"The parrot was the best actor of the lot of them, mind."

"Yeah."

"How was the weekend with your dad?"

"Okay."

I was used to Vanessa's monosyllabic style of communication, but this was ludicrously unforthcoming, even by her own standards. Under other circumstances, I would have poked her in the eye with the nonmushy end of her own banana, but I was considerate.

"Did your mum give you my message?"

"Oh, yeah. Too late to call, though. Sorry. I was really tired."

I decided a change of topic might loosen her up—you know, the stars on the periphery of your vision and all that—so I told her about the incident at Crazi-Cheep on Saturday night. I tried to make it as funny as possible. I guess, in a way, it *was* funny, but I really hammed it up, exaggerating it to bring out all the comic details. I was pleased with the way I told it. Vanessa even laughed at one stage, though I got the impression the laugh escaped unwillingly. But at least I broke through her reserve, the barrier she constructed without even being aware of it. By the time I finished, she had relaxed slightly. Physically, she was carved from a single piece of mahogany, but I could tell that emotionally she wasn't as inflexible.

I followed the hilarious incident of the runt and the frying pan with the invitation to dinner on Wednesday night and she agreed to come, though not without considerable urging after I told her Jason would probably be there. She trotted out all the reasons about not wanting to be a fifth wheel, but I managed to wear her down.

The conversation went so well I pushed my luck. The bell

had rung and we were wandering over to our legal studies class.

"Nessa?" I said. "I saw you Friday night. After the film. You were sitting on a bench by the river and you were upset. I was going to come over, but you took off. Is everything okay?"

As soon as I asked, I knew it was a mistake. I wasn't looking directly at her but I knew she stiffened. You can tell these things. And the atmosphere—I'm good at atmospheres—suddenly became arctic. It was ninety degrees in the schoolyard, but we were walking in our own refrigerated capsule. I didn't say anything else. I shoot too often and too wildly from the lip, but even I realized damage control was best achieved through silence. When Vanessa spoke, I knew she was lying. I also knew I couldn't confront her with it.

"You must have been mistaken, Calma," she said. "It wasn't me."

"Oh? Yeah. I must have been. Sorry," I replied.

We sat together in legal studies and I worked on defrosting the situation. By the end of the class I'd made some headway. We were only up to cool, but to my mind that was better than frozen.

Jason was waiting for me at the end of the day. He was smiling and leaning up against an old but neat-looking black sports car in the student car park. I couldn't help it. I gave a loud whoop and ran, dragging Vanessa behind me.

"Cool," I said, not even bothering how unoriginal I sounded. "Is this yours?"

Jason's smile broadened. He was beaming so much that if his grin got any wider the top of his head would drop off.

"Like it?" he said.

"It's great!"

"Got it yesterday. Had to go out of town, down the coast a ways."

I thumped him on the arm.

"Bastard!" I said. "So that's why you didn't come to see me?"

Jason rubbed his arm ruefully.

"God, Calma. For a chick, you pack a hell of a punch. That'll bruise."

"Good. You deserve it."

He put his arm around me.

"I know. I meant to come round. But the motor negotiations took longer than I thought. My dad and I didn't get back until ten in the evening. I was going to give you a bell, but . . . here I am. Fancy a spin?"

I'd forgotten Jason and Vanessa didn't know each other. They'd been briefly introduced at the cinema on Friday, but Vanessa was hanging back now, sidling off into the distance and giving a convincing impression of a fifth wheel. I grabbed her by the sleeve and pulled her back.

"Can Vanessa come? You remember Vanessa, from the cinema?"

Jason smiled again, all flashing white teeth and gleaming olive skin.

"Yeah, of course. There's room in the back."

Vanessa went scarlet.

**159**

"No. You guys go. I'm fine," she spluttered.

But I wasn't letting her get away with that. I had to repair the earlier damage.

"No chance. You're coming with us, isn't she, Jason?"

"Sure. Hey, what about going to Waterworld? We could get there in twenty minutes."

Now this made me more excited, if that was possible. Waterworld had only just opened a week ago, and I wanted to check it out. I'd heard it was brilliant, with scary slides and fountains and waterfalls and everything.

"Fantastic," I said. "Can we drop into Crazi-Cheep so I can get my pay and then stop off at Vanessa's place and mine to pick up bathing suits?"

"Sorted."

Vanessa continued to object, but Jason and I overrode her. The thing was, Vanessa loved swimming. It was the only thing she showed any enthusiasm for. Mention swimming and *both* her eyebrows would lift fractionally—the Vanessa equivalent of screaming "You beauty!" at the top of her lungs. I knew she really wanted to go and it was just a case of applying enough pressure.

I slung her bag into the back of the car and bundled her in after it. Jason helped me into the bucket seat at the front.

What a gentleman.

And then he went around to the driver's side and slipped into the seat without opening the door.

What a stud.

He turned the ignition key.

"Hey, matey," I said over the engine noise. "Just so you know. I am not impressed by speed, risk taking, and general dickhead driving behavior. Any of that and I'm out of the car and you're history. Okay?"

"Anything you say, Calma," he replied, putting the car in gear, releasing the clutch, and leaving the car park as if from a greased slingshot. But I didn't have to worry. Jason was a good driver and he didn't drive fast. There's something about sports cars, though, particularly convertibles, that gives the impression of speed. Perhaps it's to do with being close to the ground, but even at 30 mph I felt the exhilaration associated with extreme sports. I missed having hair. It would have been great to have had locks fluttering in the slipstream. I could have tossed my head and laughed, like they do in movies. As it was, small insects kept colliding with my scalp, like asteroids impacting the moon. They bloody hurt too.

The image of the moon bothered me. I hoped I wouldn't get out of the car with craters all over my head.

We stopped at my house first and I grabbed my suit in record time. By an amazing stroke of luck, I found it in the first drawer I opened. Given the mess in my bedroom, this was akin to finding a needle in a whole field of haystacks. Then it was off to Vanessa's house.

Mrs. Aldrick opened the door, took one look at me and Vanessa, and jumped behind a six-foot wall of sandbags positioned in the center of the living room. Well, actually, she didn't. But I was amazed, as always, by the air of terror she exuded in the most commonplace of circumstances. I didn't get time to

**161**

think about it. Vanessa grabbed her suit and a towel and then it was on to Crazi-Cheep.

Candy was chewing slowly behind the customer service desk. I wondered if she slept there, standing up in an unconscious state like horses are rumored to do, jaws moving in dreamlike rumination. Then I thought, *Who cares?* and got my paycheck. It was pitifully thin but at least it made me feel independent. My first wages! I couldn't wait to spend the lot, even if that would only take five minutes. Provided I was frugal.

I was approaching the automatic doors when a woman grabbed me by the arm. It took a few seconds to place her. It was my first customer, the woman I had overcharged. I remembered the kindness of her face and the infectious laughter. She wasn't laughing now. Her face was crinkled into lines of worry and she held on to my arm with a firm, almost desperate grip.

"Oh, Calma," she said. "How are you feeling?"

I was puzzled and it must have shown on my face because she continued.

"I read about it in the newspaper. How dreadful. And how brave, the way you tackled him, a crazed gunman, with just a frying pan. Are you okay?"

"I'm fine," I replied. "We're trained for this sort of thing. It comes between the session on how to stack spaghetti and the one about mopping up milk spills. 'Methods of disarming homicidal maniacs with domestic appliances.' "

I regretted the remark as soon as it passed my lips. She was so nice she didn't deserve sarcasm. But sometimes I can't help myself. I needn't have worried, though. Her eyes sparkled with humor and she laughed. The entire store stopped and stared and I noticed some of the customers were laughing too. Even Candy, not known for a well-developed sense of humor—*any* sense of humor, come to think of it—twisted her mouth in a passable imitation of a smile. And *they* didn't know what they were laughing at.

"I'm so sorry," I said, "but I've got people waiting for me. I must dash."

The woman wiped her eyes with one hand and waved at me with the other.

"Go on, go on," she said between gasps of laughter. "I'm just glad you're all right."

Just occasionally, you need your faith in human nature restored. I thought as much as I got into the car, still chuckling, and Jason pulled out of the car park. Out of the corner of my eye, I noticed a small, balding man waving. Then he was gone and in three seconds I had forgotten he was ever there.

We headed off along the coast road. It was one of those days when it felt good to be alive. The sky was powdery blue, with little wisps of cloud arranged artistically for maximum aesthetic effect. The ocean was a glorious green with feathers of white breakers. A warm wind buffeted our faces and my skin tingled in the sun. It was lovely.

Talking was difficult. The wind whipped the words away as soon as they left my mouth. So I leaned close to Jason's ear and yelled. I could smell his skin, earthy, with the faintest tinge of aftershave, and my blood pumped with dangerous excitement.

I asked if he could make it for the meal on Wednesday with me, the Fridge, and Vanessa. He frowned a little, eyes fixed on the road.

"What's the occasion?" he yelled.

"My birthday," I screamed back.

"Shite," he bellowed. "Just my luck to get a girlfriend a few days before her birthday. Bad financial planning, that."

"Maybe you should dump me on Tuesday and then get back together on Thursday," I suggested.

"Hey," he said, "good thinking, Calma. I like the cut of your jib."

"Course," I continued, "you'd be financially in the black, but emotionally deep in the brown stuff."

"Yeah. Point taken." He took a sharp corner and the muscles in his forearm flexed as he moved the wheel. Back on the straight, he turned his eyes toward me. "I'd love to come. I'm supposed to be working, but I'll get out of it."

There was silence for a while and then he spoke again.

"Meeting your mother? It's not the first step to marriage, is it?"

"I've no idea," I said. "You could *try* proposing to her, but it's risky on the first date, and anyway, I'm not sure she's your type."

I felt happy. I hadn't felt really happy for a long time and I was enjoying it. I didn't want the drive to end. I could have stayed there forever, yelling stupid comments into Jason's ear, the wind against my head, the sun and the clouds and the sea spread before me, as if for my eyes only.

*    *    *

Waterworld was awesome. It was huge, stretching out over acres against the backdrop of the sea. From the entrance it seemed to go on forever, as if there was no boundary between the main pool and the limitless ocean. There wasn't just one pool, either. There were four. One was a regular lap pool, with people relentlessly swimming back and forth. There was another place for small kids, with a fountain and all kinds of play equipment. Then there was a huge, circular pool with a spa where families were hanging out, splashing around, and duck-diving. It was the fourth pool that attracted our attention most, however. It was the biggest of the lot and it had diving boards, water chutes, slides, and big corkscrew slippery dips that started way up in the heavens and flung you, screaming and yelling, into a froth of bubbles at the deep end. The three of us didn't have to say anything. We knew where we would be spending the rest of the afternoon.

Nessa and I got changed, took a quick shower in our suits, and headed toward the slides. Jason emerged from the men's changing rooms a minute later. I was relieved he wasn't wearing a Speedo. I can't stand Speedos. It's almost impossible to keep your eyes off them, even—especially—when you can't bear to look. If you want my opinion, Mother Nature demonstrated a fine sense of the absurd when she designed that portion of the male anatomy.

Nonetheless, I wasn't averse to checking out his general physique, though this wasn't as easy as it might sound. I mean, you can't say something like, *Hang on, Jason. Take a few steps*

**165**

*back while I scan your body for imperfections.* You have to stare into someone's eyes while at the same time trying to check out the rest of their body without them noticing. I suppose you could pretend you'd just seen a UFO and, while he's peering into the sky and shielding his eyes with his hands, have a damn good perv. But this seemed lacking in finesse to me, so I waited until he swept his gaze around the pool.

It was worth the wait, let me tell you. He had one of those wiry bodies, all subtle muscle definition with a flat stomach and a cute belly button that stuck out. His skin was a beautiful olive shade all over, with none of those nasty, pasty patches where the sun hasn't reached. It was all I could do not to drool.

Anyway, I was aware he was doing exactly the same thing to me. When I pondered the assembled multitudes, I could tell his eyes were darting all over me. Mind you, he had less to go on than I did. I don't wear bikinis, mainly because, as I might have mentioned earlier, I have boobs the size of a medium family saloon. They don't look good in bikinis. They don't look good in anything. Keep everything safely gathered—that's always been my motto.

Even in a one-piece, I attracted attention as I walked along the edge of the pool. Maybe it was my shaved head. I probably gave the impression of training so seriously I was prepared to go bald to cut one-hundredth of a second off my personal best. If that was people's impression, I quickly dispelled it once in the water. I'm more of the float-around-the-pool-like-a-large-inflatable type than a serious swimmer.

I'm not like Vanessa. She's part fish. On dry land, she's out of her element, all languid movement, like a pale snail. Throw her in water, however, and she's transformed. She jets through the wet stuff like a torpedo, tumble-turns at the end of the lap, and pushes off. If I tried a tumble turn, I'd dash my head against the tiles and need resuscitation. I watched Vanessa swim and wanted to check behind her ears for gills. She was beautiful.

We had a fantastic time. The best was going on the long slide. We climbed steps for what seemed forever, and when we got to the top, it was all I could do to stop clinging to the rail or sinking to my knees in panic. I'm talking high! Mind you, the view was brilliant. The pool was laid out beneath us like a blue carpet, small figures frolicking in the water. Then we had to get into the mouth of a huge chute, with water churning around, and we were swept into darkness. The first time I tried it, Vanessa and Jason nearly had to pry my fingers away from the side of the chute with a chisel. I was petrified. And then I was plunging, whirling in the void, sweeping around bends, legs flinging up into the air in the most inelegant fashion, before I was catapulted into the pool, water rushing and roaring in my ears. I was suspended for a while in the calm blue before popping to the surface like a demented cork. I screamed the whole time. Including underwater, which explained my purple-faced coughing fit by the side of the pool.

I leaped out and raced up the steps for another go.

After a couple of hours, the crowds thinned as people went home, I supposed, for their dinners. Night fell, floodlights came on, and the whole place was even more beautiful. The water reflected the lights; it was alive with shimmering flashes. Jason came up behind me in the deep end and gave me a dunking. I bobbed to the surface, spluttering, and he wrapped his arms around me. He kissed me briefly, his lips on mine like an electric shock, but I pulled away. It didn't feel right somehow. Not there. Not then.

Eventually, we got out of the pool and sat at a table in the café area, with Cokes and packets of chips. I was starving from all that sun and water and laughter and exercise. Vanessa's face glowed. She looked happy and animated. I felt infused with warmth, for her, for Jason. I tell you, things didn't get much better than this.

I should have known it couldn't last.

Jason glanced at his watch but we already knew it was time for home. Reluctantly I gathered my things together and Nessa and I took off for the changing rooms.

I got under the shower in one cubicle, while Nessa disappeared into another. I felt I could not get enough water over me, standing there, face upturned to the jet. I rubbed my hands over my skin, the faint smell of chlorine like a perfume. Of course, in the excitement and the rush I hadn't brought any shower gel. I wondered if Nessa had been more organized.

I stepped from the shower and tapped against the door of her cubicle.

"Nessa," I said.

I hadn't realized the cubicle wasn't locked. The door swung open.

"You don't have any shower gel, by any . . ."

She was naked. I apologized as she turned her back to me. I pulled the cubicle door closed.

I felt sick to my stomach. Not because I'd seen her naked. But because I'd seen the damage. Cuts, welts, and scratches on her stomach, and one bright laceration at the top of her left hip. They burned in my brain. Injuries hidden from the world, covered even by a bathing suit.

I went to the toilet and threw up. The shower was still running. I don't think she heard me.

No one said much on the drive back. I sat quietly in the front seat and tilted my head toward the stars. I stared at one spot in the sky. I called it Vanessa. Before long, the periphery of my vision was filled with spots of light. They began to make a pattern.

# Chapter 20

## A different kind of statement

There was a message on the answering machine when I got home. The police. They wanted me to come to the station to make a statement about the attempted robbery at Crazi-Cheep. I called back. They asked if I could come as soon as possible. The Fridge wasn't home, so I took the bus. The last thing I felt like doing was sitting at home. I welcomed the distraction. The police told me the lateness of the hour made no difference. There was someone there who could take a statement. The cop shop didn't close.

I went through the doors of the station and gave my name at reception. The officer told me to take a seat, that someone would attend to me soon. I sat in a torn vinyl chair and studied posters of missing persons. Last seen in Townsville in 1995. Parents anxious for information. A wife who went to the local shops in 2001 for tea bags and had never returned. Children who went to parties and were never seen again. So many lives with holes in them.

Eventually, I was taken by a female police officer into an interview room. She chatted in a friendly fashion until a plainclothes officer arrived. He asked me questions about the attempted robbery, while the other officer jotted notes on a pad. The whole thing must have taken about half an hour. When we were done, the note taker left the room, presumably to type up my statement. I sat in the chair, nursing a dull headache.

The plainclothes officer talked, but I didn't pay attention. To be honest, I didn't want to look at him. I could feel his eyes, like a stain on my body, as if he was mentally undressing me. It had happened before. I suppose it will happen again. It makes me feel sick. In other circumstances I would have reacted. In the past I had humiliated the sleazebags whose gaze lingered on me longer than necessary. But I wasn't in the mood today, so I kept my eyes down and answered his questions in monosyllables.

The female officer returned. I signed the statement. I was taken back to reception and told I might have to appear in court as a witness, unless the guy pleaded guilty. They'd be in contact.

I caught the bus home. The Fridge still wasn't in.

I was desperately tired. All that sunshine and water and exercise. I went to bed.

I didn't sleep all night. I don't think I even closed my eyes.

# Chapter 21

## Time for action

Tell me I got it wrong. Please.

This is the way I thought it through. Not so much a logical argument, more a series of images that coalesced. Stars on the edge.

Mrs. Aldrick. Nervous. Not a comic figure, after all. Not someone to laugh at or make stupid jokes about how she seemed constantly on the verge of panic. No. Someone with a history. Someone who had been made that way by years of cruelty. Someone who, even though she no longer lived with the source of terror, had it ingrained in her responses. A door slamming, a voice raised. Enough to make her blood race, her nerves twitch. Seeking a place to hide, even years later. Someone who knew better than to give out unauthorized phone numbers.

Vanessa. Withdrawn, shy, no confidence. Reluctant to share feelings. Scared when the weekend for her visit with her dad was approaching. Tears on a bench. Afterward, more withdrawn than normal. Aggressive, distracted—sometimes at the same time. Cuts and scratches in places where cuts and scratches should not be. Fresh wounds. Recent wounds. Inflicted in areas normally hidden.

Tell me I got it wrong. Please.

At some time, around six in the morning—the darkness was starting to dissolve—I stopped crying. I wasn't aware I had begun, but my pillow was wet. I took a deep, shuddering breath and something amazing happened. The sadness and feeling of powerlessness disappeared and were replaced by a knot of anger. Sheer rage was lodged between my ribs and I knew nothing would get rid of it—nothing except finding a man whose name I didn't know, whose appearance was a mystery. A man about whom I knew nothing, except that he lived somewhere in the city and he was Vanessa's father.

I needed to tell him a few things.

I went to school, though I didn't feel like it. I was exhausted, physically and emotionally. There was nothing I could say to Vanessa, either. I knew it instinctively. If I tried to broach the subject, she'd clam up. God knows she clammed up even when the conversation wasn't threatening.

I tried to keep up my spirits, if only for her sake, to offer a veneer of normality. The hardest part was resurrecting a sense of humor that felt dead within me. But that was the Calma persona now, so I worked at it throughout the day. Luckily, most of the time I was fending off taunts from assorted drop-kicks, so I was able to indulge in the kind of barbed humor that was second nature to me anyway.

Examples?

"Hey, Calma. If I get you a frying pan, will you bash the principal?"

"Beat it, Jamie."

Okay, so I wasn't in the greatest form.

During the morning break, I decided that moping around, trying to dredge up a personality, was not the way to go. I needed action. So I went to the office and borrowed their Yellow Pages. It took some finding, but eventually I got the number of the Office of Births, Deaths, and Marriages at the Department of Justice. Students can't make phone calls from the school office—not unless we have written permission from the principal, both assistant principals, and the director of education, and are in receipt of a decree in Latin signed by the Pope—so I got some change and went to the public phone across the road.

Students are not supposed to use that either, because we're not allowed to leave the school grounds unless we have written permission from the principal.

I dialed the number and a bored voice told me I had reached the Office of Births, Deaths, and Marriages, that it was a good morning, that her name was Julie, and that she was prepared to help me. As it turned out, she got at least one of those things wrong. I started the conversation brightly enough, mind.

"G'day, Julie," I said. "I am hoping you can help me. I'm

trying to track down the name of a person. The only information I've got is that he has a daughter, whose name I could give you, but it probably wouldn't help because she has taken on her mother's maiden name, since the guy I'm looking for divorced her mother."

"I beg your pardon?"

I was aware I hadn't explained very well, so I tried another tack.

"Do you keep records of divorces?"

"Certainly not," said Julie, in a tone of voice usually reserved for responses to dirty phone calls.

"How about birth certificates?" It occurred to me that, knowing Vanessa's birth date, I might be able to track down a copy of her certificate, and this would lead to the name of her father.

"Well, yes. That's why we are called the Office of Births, Deaths, and Marriages."

"Excellent," I replied. "Tell me, Julie, are these birth certificates available for public scrutiny?"

"No."

"Would you care to clarify that?"

"You want me to clarify the word *no*?"

"If you're capable. You see, Julie, the word *no* seems to imply that your office is merely a repository of information. It suggests filing cabinets full of dusty documents no one is allowed to see. Why bother even having a phone number? Why bother having a receptionist, come to that, unless your only function is to stonewall inquiries?"

There was a sharp intake of breath. I got the impression I hadn't made a new friend here. When she spoke again, the earpiece frosted over and a chilly mist numbed my ear.

"Access to birth certificates is only available for the person named on the certificate or, under certain circumstances, members of the immediate family. *Are* you immediate family?"

"Not in the limited technical sense."

"Is there anything else I can be of assistance with?"

"I find that inconceivable. Thank you. It's been a rare pleasure and privilege chatting with you, Julie. Have a nice day."

Okay, so I might have handled the whole process better. I had been entertaining images of going into a record office and sorting through ledgers while some rosy-cheeked old biddy offered me cups of tea and assorted chocolate cookies. That was the way it worked in detective books. Clearly, real life wasn't so easy.

I wasn't giving up, mind. When the going gets tough, old Calma digs deep. I walked back to the school, thinking furiously. I was so lost in my own world that I wasn't aware of Jamie Gallagher when he fell in beside me.

"Hey, Calma. I'm on the Year Ten fund-raising committee. For a gold coin donation, I could give your head a wash and full wax. Or do you think that's robbery? What do you say?"

I stopped and stared at him. Now, Jamie's face could not, under most circumstances, be termed a source of inspiration. Perspiration, possibly. Desperation, probably. But an idea flashed into my mind. It was simple. It was brilliant. It would work.

Maybe.

And all I needed to do was manipulate Jamie Gallagher into behaving like a dickhead. A bit like asking a dog to bark, or a fish to swim, or a receptionist to be unhelpful.

"Jamie," I said pleasantly, "you are, without doubt, a loathsome, suppurating pimple on the backside of humanity."

"Oh, yeah?" he sneered.

"Indeed," I replied. "I have the utmost confidence that, faced with the simplest challenge to your intelligence and enterprise, you would fail spectacularly. In fact, I'd put money on it."

"Oh, yeah?" he sneered, but I got the impression I'd lost him completely. He knew he was being insulted but wasn't sure how.

"For example," I said. "I'd be willing to bet ten dollars you couldn't do something really simple, something any idiot could do."

"Oh, yeah? Like what?" He obviously felt relieved to be back on board the conversation.

I shrugged.

"Oh, I don't know." I pretended to give it thought. "All right," I continued. "How about this? I'll bet you ten bucks you can't get Miss Moil to leave her office at lunchtime."

Miss Moil was the assistant principal and in charge of scheduling and student records. She was a nice old stick, but one of those people who doesn't have a life outside work. You got the impression she was chained to her desk, and the only way she'd leave the school would be in a pine box. She should have retired some time in the 1970s but still hung around like a stubborn cobweb. I got along well with her because, despite the air of decrepitude, she had a dry sense of humor.

"That's easy," said Jamie.

"Prove it," I said.

"I just have to get her out of her office?" His face was furrowed while he looked for the catch. "And you'll give me ten bucks?"

"Okay," I said. "If you think that's too easy, let's make it more interesting. You have to get her to leave not just her office but the administration building. And you have to do it at exactly twelve-thirty. If you can, I'll give you ten bucks. In fact, if you fail, you don't have to pay me anything. Ten bucks against nothing, that's the bet."

"If I don't get her out the building at twelve-thirty, I won't owe you nothing, but if I do, you'll give me ten bucks?"

"Come on, Jamie. This isn't quantum physics. Deal or not?"

"Deal."

I tell you. Sometimes it's too easy.


Miss Moil gave me a big grin when I entered her office at 12:25 exactly. I was relieved to see she was alone.

"Calma Harrison! How are you, dear?"

"Good, Miss Moil. How are you?"

"Can't complain. Wouldn't do me much good, anyway. No one listens. Now, what can I do for you?"

She was sitting in front of her computer. She was always sitting in front of her computer.

"Oh, my mum wanted me to give you another contact number. She's got a new cell and thought the school might want it, in case of an emergency."

"Excellent. We're always keen to update our database. Sometimes we have terrible trouble tracking people down."

She tapped a few keys on her computer and brought up a window with a user name and password box. A few moments later she was into student records. I peered over her shoulder as she entered the first four letters of my last name into a search box. A window appeared with my name in the top left corner. All my details were there: address, date of birth, contact details. Miss Moil clicked the cursor on the box next to the Fridge's name.

"Right, dear," she said. "And the number?"

Then the door burst open and Jamie Gallagher rushed in. His timing was perfect. I didn't want to lie to Miss Moil any more than necessary.

I'll give Jamie this. He had hidden depths. Who would have believed he could act? Yet there he was, all sweaty, panicky, and exuding concern. Robert De Niro could have taken his correspondence course.

"Miss Moil, come quick," he panted. "Daniel O'Leary has Jeff Brown around the neck. I think he's going to kill him."

I felt sorry for Miss Moil. She's not the quickest mover in the world, partly because she is horrendously overweight.

"Oh, my," she puffed, and pried her bulk out of her chair. Jamie was already halfway down the corridor, gesturing wildly, urging her on. Miss Moil waddled after him, patting herself on the chest with one pudgy hand, small sounds of concern and distress fading with her footsteps. I went to work.

It took less than a minute. I clicked the back button on the window and then entered "Aldr" in the search box. By the time Miss Moil returned to her office, I was long gone, and the window displaying the details of "Harrison, Calma" filled her screen.

Just occasionally, life provides you with an unexpected bonus. Jamie Gallagher was clearly a gifted actor. Unfortunately he forgot one important thing: if you are going to tell an enormous whopper, then it's a good idea to cover yourself. When Miss Moil finally emerged into the sunshine, sweating and doubtless on the point of a coronary, there was no fight going on anywhere. The supposed combatants weren't even in school. They had skipped and were, even as Jamie was leading Miss Moil up the garden path, engaging in minor shoplifting at the local mall.

When pressed for further information, Jamie Gallagher was at a loss. When accused of making a malicious false report, he had no answers.

He didn't get his ten dollars.

He got five days' suspension.

I, meanwhile, got a name and a phone number.

# Chapter 22

## Facing the demon

The phone book was no help, so I was forced to call. The first couple of times I tried I got an answering machine. It was third time lucky.

"Hello?"

"Is that Mr. Michael Collins?"

"Speaking. Who's this?"

"I'm the assistant principal at Vanessa's school. I'm sorry to bother you, Mr. Collins, but we are updating our database and don't have an address for you. I'm sure you will want to receive copies of Vanessa's reports at the end of the semester."

"Oh . . . yeah. I guess. Well . . . okay. It's unit five, thirty-seven Smith Street, in the city."

"Thank you so much, Mr. Collins."

"Who did you say you were again?"

"Ms. Pharcue, Mr. Collins. Pharcue." I hung up.

With all this activity, I got little done at school that day.

When the bell rang, I walked with Vanessa to the parking lot, but there was no sign of Jason or his car. Pity.

We walked home. Nessa was distracted, but she was always distracted—only the degree varied. She went into her house without saying a word; I wasn't disappointed. I had a job to do and figured it was best to get it over and done with as soon as possible. Frankly, if I thought too long, I'd lose impetus. It's all very well to plan, but I had reached the confrontation stage and it seemed much more difficult. So I strode home, trying not to think. I kept repeating to myself, "You're mean, you're tough, you're streetwise. You're mean, you're tough . . ."

> Calma Harrison threw herself into the battered chair and removed the bottle of Jack Daniel's from the top drawer of her desk. Unscrewing the cap with her teeth, she took a slug and reached into her pocket for a cigar. This was going to be an ugly job, but she was used to ugly jobs. A match materialized between finger and thumb and she scratched it against her head.
>
> Only when the cigar was lit did she lean forward, pick up the phone, and dial.
>
> "Get over here now," she growled into the mouthpiece. "I need wheels."
>
> Calma replaced the handset and looked out the window. The city, choked with smog, lay before her like a corpse in a smoke-filled strip joint. It crawled with low-life, sleazy scumbags, like fleas on a mangy cur. It was tough, like old

*leather, but Calma was a broad who was no stranger to toughness. Her head reflected the city lights, like an eight-ball in a laser factory. She sighed, like a stiff croaking its last breath, and stretched. Her muscles creaked like an overly elaborate simile.*

*Jason entered. He was looking sharp, as always. Calma glanced at him and wondered, not for the first time, whether he could be trusted. He was a wiseguy, a kid off the streets, a punk on the make, a player, a hood.*

*"Are you packing?" asked Calma.*

*"Is it vacation time, boss?" he asked.*

*"No. Are you packing a piece?"*

*"Of what?"*

*"A rod. Are you packing a rod?"*

*"Fishing?"*

*Calma sighed. Maybe he wasn't such a wiseguy after all. Never mind. She had her own piece, a Glock snub-nosed automatic, in her garter belt. The squirrel she was after was a bad squirrel, a dangerous squirrel, a squirrel who wouldn't give up his nuts without a fight.*

*"We're going after a squirrel," she said. "That's why I need your ride. We'll take him out in his own crib." Jason took out his A-Z guide of tough street talk and thumbed through the pages. Calma groaned. He should have known this stuff by heart. If he failed his gumshoe exams at the end of the month, she wasn't going to take responsibility. She wasn't going to be the fall guy, the patsy . . .*

The trouble was, I didn't feel tough, despite the mantra. In fact, if I have to be honest, I was less private eye and more primary reader.

> See Calma. See the car. Calma gets in the car. See Calma get in the car. Clever Calma.
>
> Calma goes to the house. Calma knocks on the door. See Calma knock on the door.
>
> Calma talks to the man. The man punches Calma. See the man punch Calma.
>
> Calma is in big poo-poo. See Calma in poo-poo.
>
> Run, Calma, run.

The Fridge wasn't home, of course. There had been more recorded sightings of the yeti than there had been of her in the last decade. I was considering getting a life-sized cardboard cut-out of her to leave around the house.

The two hours home alone gave me the opportunity to think before Jason turned up at five-thirty. I tried to rehearse what I was going to say to Vanessa's father, but it was no use. I mean, what can you do? Smile and say, "Excuse me, Mr. Collins. I'm sorry to bother you, but I have reason to believe you are abusing your daughter. Now, if it's not a rude question, I wonder if you would mind stopping this forthwith. At your own convenience, naturally"?

Each scenario I acted out seemed impossible. So I decided to play it by ear. What if I was wrong, though? That bothered me as well. Vanessa hadn't said anything. What if she had fallen down the stairs at home and I was going to accuse an entirely innocent man of an appalling crime? How could I look Vanessa in the face again? Where would that leave our relationship? Down the toilet, that's where.

The more I thought, the more tempted I was to forget the whole thing. Inaction was such an alluring option. But what was it someone had once said? All that's required for evil to flourish is for good people to do nothing. Something like that. And I trusted my feelings. I *knew* Vanessa's injuries couldn't have been inflicted by accident. I *had* to do something.

I just wasn't looking forward to it.

I also thought about the Fridge. My sneaking around had come up with absolutely nothing. Still, *she* knew that *I* knew she was keeping a secret. What's more, she was going to tell me about it. I resolved to demand a full revelation the next time I saw her. I was tired of lies and half-truths.

Then there was my father. He wanted to tell me something too. It was ironic. I was desperate for information from the Fridge but she was saying nothing. I didn't want information from my own father and he was desperate to give it. It's a funny old world, isn't it? I remembered the attempt he had made at the supermarket, just before the thieving, gun-toting runt had arrived on the scene. I remembered also my feelings after my father left Crazi-Cheep. That small, fleeting twinge of regret.

Maybe I had been too hard on him. After all, the nastiness was in the past. By spurning him so completely and ruthlessly now, I was giving the impression he still had the means to inflict suffering. If I treated him politely, as a stranger, then I would show him he no longer had that power. In fact, politeness would be more humiliating for him. And what if he *was* going to beg for forgiveness, try to worm his way back into our affections? That didn't mean he would succeed. I could hear him out and then politely tell him to go forth and multiply. It was the mature way of proceeding.

That left Jason. I couldn't tell him about Vanessa. I couldn't tell anyone about Vanessa, let alone a guy I had known for about five minutes. Yet I wanted him to be there when I confronted her father. As moral and, maybe, physical support. Was that fair? Probably not, I thought. But perhaps it would be a test of his loyalty and good faith, to do something because I asked him, without reasons or explanations. Hmmm. I suspected I was rationalizing my own dubious behavior, but I couldn't see a way round that either. I liked Jason. A lot. But I didn't know him at all. I hoped I would get the opportunity when all this was done.

I tell you, with this degree of thinking going on, it was a muddle-headed Calma who opened the door to greet Jason when he turned up at five-thirty.

"Where do you want to go?" Jason asked, jingling the car keys in his hand and looking preternaturally spunky. "The world is our oyster. Provided we're back by seven-thirty. There are highlights of the Premiership weekend fixtures and Liverpool kicked butt."

"Two hours to explore the oyster of the world and then

back to watch soccer? Boy, you're a real smooth operator, Jason. You could charm the birds out of the trees, you know?"

His face fell.

"We don't have to watch football," he said earnestly. "Not if you don't fancy it."

I squeezed his arm.

"I'm kidding," I said. "I'd love to watch soccer with you. There are some pressing questions you can answer about gonads, the offside trap, and the role of flying snot."

Jason parked downtown and suggested we go to one of the cafés on the main strip. I suggested a walk. I had to get this done. I couldn't sip hot chocolate and make small talk. My stomach was doing flips and they were getting worse the longer I delayed.

I led Jason up Smith Street, a road running parallel to the main street. It was a good neighborhood. Expensive condos, with balconies and views over the city and ocean. Carefully tended palms arched over us as we walked. There was a chatter of lorikeets in a nearby tree. It was peaceful.

Number thirty-seven was a block of apartments like the others, well-tended, with gleaming screen doors and taut awnings. I was dismayed to see the entrance to the apartments was through a locked gate—one that operated electronically, with an intercom. I didn't want to buzz Mr. Collins. I wouldn't know what to say. *Can you let me in so I can insult you?*

As it turned out, my luck was in. Or out, depending on

your viewpoint. A woman came down the steps of the apartment block and pointed a remote control at the gate, which slid noiselessly open on its tracks.

I grabbed Jason's hand and we ran the last twenty yards before the gate closed. If I'd thought about it, I'd have worried that Jason would be getting seriously bothered by my habit of running for no discernible reason.

We managed to slip inside the gate with seconds to spare. Jason gave me an odd look. His cigarette had fallen out of his mouth and he glanced back at it, smoldering on the road, with longing and regret. I made a resolution that when this was done, I'd turn my attention to his unsavory addiction.

"What's going on, Calma?" he said.

"Nothing," I replied. "I just have to make a quick visit. Stand here. Don't move. Watch me at all times."

The door to apartment five was on the ground floor, facing the gate. Convenient. Jason was clearly puzzled, but I didn't allow him the opportunity to give me the third degree. Firming up my resolution, I marched to the door and knocked loudly.

I am not ashamed to admit it. I was praying no one would be in.

The door opened almost immediately and a man filled the available space. I opened my mouth to speak but forgot how you go about it. Nerves, probably. All I could manage was a strangled grunt.

While I waited to see if my nervous system could resurrect

the correct procedure for speech, I took the opportunity to examine him more closely. He was in his forties and his most distinguishable feature was long, wavy hair. It had probably been blond at some stage but now it was streaked with grey.

The word is *distinguished.* He had a Richard Gere look—that old actor who still manages to give women over the age of fifty palpitations. The Fridge would probably have been putty in his hands, but I thought he was in desperate need of a haircut. If I got the opportunity, I'd recommend Allessandro's. Tearing my gaze from his hair, I met his eyes. They were blue and weak and sitting too close to his nose. Maybe it was my imagination, but I could see cruelty swimming just beneath the surface.

He was well dressed and had a fairly good physique. He gave the impression of having lifted weights, but in the past. Even so, he could probably blow me away with a sneeze. Suddenly, the presence of Jason behind me didn't offer any comfort. It felt like I was confronting a charging rhinoceros with a koala for backup.

There was something familiar about him too. Maybe it was the family resemblance to Vanessa. There was something about the set of his eyes and the way his nose turned up slightly. Plus he had freckles.

All this observation took place in less than a second. I tried the mouth again and, to my surprise, it had finally reported for duty.

"Mr. Collins?" I said.

"Yes?"

This was my chance to say something like, *I was wondering if I could interest you in a time-share opportunity in a new building development on the Gaza Strip.* But I didn't take it.

"I'm a friend of your daughter. Vanessa Aldrick."

"She's not here."

"I know. It was you I wanted to see."

"What for?"

"I wanted to tell you, Mr. Collins, that I know what you've been doing to Vanessa. And I'm telling you to stop it. She doesn't know I'm here. She doesn't even know I know about it. She kept it to herself. But I *do* know. And if you lay a finger on her ever again, then you will be sorry. Keep away from her, Mr. Collins."

I didn't have a clue what would happen next. To be honest, I was so glad to get the speech off my chest, even if it was a crappy, weak-kneed speech, that I didn't care too much. If he punched me, so be it. At least I'd had my say.

He didn't punch me, though. He stared at me. The feeling of familiarity grew. Something about his expression. He gave a tight smile. It was scarier than a punch.

"Tell me, Calma," he said finally. "What makes you think you can come to my house and make wild, reckless accusations? What gives you the right?"

I straightened my back and kept my eyes fixed on his. I couldn't let him see any weakness. Did he call me Calma?

"I will not hesitate to call the police, Mr. Collins. Even

without Vanessa's knowledge or permission, I *will* notify the authorities."

The thin smile was still there, and when he spoke, it was with a terrifying softness.

"Well, that should be interesting. You see, I *am* the police, Miss Harrison. I'm surprised you don't remember me."

And that was the moment it all fell into place. The plainclothes officer in the interview room. The guy who was mentally undressing me while his colleague was off typing up my statement about the robbery at Crazi-Cheep. The realization clubbed me on the back of the head. It left me feeling sick, angry, and defeated. I stared blankly at him, only dimly aware of a woman's voice coming from the depths of the apartment.

"Mike? Who is it?"

Vanessa's dad turned to the side and I could see into the room behind. This whole experience had made me sick, but things suddenly took a turn for the worse. The Fridge walked out from a room and moved toward the front door, her expression changing from mild concern to shock as she recognized me.

I turned and ran.

See Calma run.

# Chapter 23
## Trying to move the Fridge

I sat on the floor in front of the television, watching a program on the mating habits of the aesthetically challenged lesser spotted newt. The male of the species, despite its appearance, didn't have problems attracting females. It cavorted around, waving disfigured limbs and inflating cheeks until it was touch-and-go whether its head would explode, and the females were falling over themselves, getting all hot and bothered and clearly thinking, *Phwoar, what a stud!* It's a strange business, nature.

Mind you, there were boys in my year who were similarly hideous yet also had no problem scoring.

I was waiting for the Fridge to get home.

## Fact File

*Common name:* The Fridge

*Scientific name: Rustus westinghousius*

*Habitat:* Not often found in domestic houses, despite its common name, the *Rustus westinghousius* is most comfortable in undesirable places of employment, where it will remain for long periods of time, often to the detriment of its offspring. An elusive creature, it can occasionally be sighted during those infrequent moments when it rests.

*Mating habits:* Mates once and then gives up the whole business as a bad job (see *Baldus shortarsius*).However, recent research indicates its libido can hibernate for years, springing back to life when placed in close proximity to a hairy slimeball.

*Appearance:* Careworn, solid, given to dowdy outfits from cheap department stores, and in desperate need of a makeover.

*Toxicity:* Can occasionally paralyze with one blow of its tongue at distances of up to twenty yards, but generally harmless.

*Status:* Deeply worrying.

Jason had come round, but I'd refused to answer the door.

After the grisly appearance of the Fridge at the home of Vanessa's father, I'd simply run. I couldn't remember pushing past Jason at the gate. I can't even remember how I'd got through the gate. Maybe I'd vaulted it. Maybe I'd run right through it, like they do in cartoons. All I could recollect was sitting at the side of a road, head in hands, lungs screaming for air. People walked past me like I was invisible.

Eventually I got the bus home. I still didn't have keys, but there was a window round the back that was slightly open and I wriggled in. Jason turned up half an hour later. I wasn't ready to talk to him, though I knew he deserved an explanation. It would have to wait.

The phone rang a couple of times and I heard the click of the answering machine. Eventually, in case it was the Fridge calling, I went and played back the messages. Two. Both from Jason. Both asking that I call him as soon as possible. I turned down the volume and went back to the living room. Waited.

I was angry. I had plenty to be angry about. Nothing was working out at all. Everything was falling apart. And at the center of the chaos was the Fridge and Vanessa's dad. The trouble was, I didn't have much in the way of hard information. All I had were questions. What was going on between them? Was it romance? How could the Fridge, even with her tragic history of choosing the wrong guy, go for someone like that? And what if I was wrong about Vanessa's dad? There was no evidence. Nothing, as the saying goes, that would stand up in a court of law. All I had were feelings. The sensation when I felt his eyes running over my body in the police station. The coldness when he looked at me outside the apartment. Scratches on his daughter that could have happened in a number of different ways but which *felt* wrong. The atmosphere of nervousness in Vanessa's house, a chill history of repression and violence you could taste.

Only feelings. But sometimes that's enough. The feelings swirled in my head now, dark clouds building to a thunderhead. And one thought circled, again and again, splitting the brooding darkness like a flash of lightning. The Fridge had seen me at the apartment. She had seen me running. But that had been two hours ago. Didn't I matter to her at all? By the time I heard tires on the driveway, the clunk of the car door closing, and the grate of her key in the lock, I was a tight ball of resentment. I didn't get up. I stared at the television screen, though I'd long since stopped watching. There was an explosion bottled within and I knew the slightest thing would trigger it.

I sensed the Fridge behind me but didn't turn.

"It's about time we had a talk," she said.

I pressed a button on the remote and the screen blinked into darkness. There was silence. I got up from the floor and sat in a chair. I didn't look at her. The Fridge slung a bag off her shoulder and sat down wearily in the chair opposite. She sighed and rubbed at her eyes with both knuckles. I could pick up a lot from the edges of my vision.

"What's going on, Calma?" she said eventually.

"You tell me. I'm in the dark. Just where you want me to be."

"Don't be absurd. I haven't got time for stupidity."

The trigger had been squeezed. I stood up.

"No, of course you haven't," I said. "You never have time. It's in very short supply. Hey, if you've got somewhere to go, don't let me keep you. I never have in the past."

"I didn't mean—"

"Yes, you did, Mum. You did." I was pacing now. I needed movement. Energy sparked from me and I couldn't control it. "It's exactly what you mean. And I'm supposed to be grateful you can spare me a few precious moments. I'm your daughter, for Christ's sake. Your daughter. What am I supposed to do? Make an appointment?"

I couldn't stop the tears pricking my eyes. I hated that. It made me angrier.

"Calma, you're right. You're right. I'm sorry. I didn't mean it the way it sounded. All right?"

I kept pacing, but the Fridge was at the center of my vision. She seemed smaller somehow. Maybe it was the size of my anger that made her appear that way. I forced my tears to stop.

"I'm not going anywhere, okay?" she continued. "Not until we've talked everything out. That's a promise. I know I haven't been around enough. I know I should have talked to you before. You deserve that. I'm sorry. All I can say is I'm sorry. Can we talk, Calma? Please?"

I didn't say anything as I paced. Apologies are so annoying. They chip away at your anger. I let the silence stretch. The Fridge leaned back in her chair and scratched at the palm of one hand, her eyes downcast. Little lines of worry were etched into her forehead.

"I've been seeing Mike for about three weeks now. I wanted to tell you about it. I was going to tell you about it. Tonight, in fact."

I snorted.

"It's the truth," she said.

"Out of curiosity," I said, "why didn't you tell me before? I mean, it's a fairly big deal, isn't it? I'm assuming that when you say 'seeing,' you mean a romance. Yeah?"

The Fridge didn't reply and my stomach lurched at the tacit admission. I hurried on.

"So what is it about me that meant you couldn't say anything? Come on, Mum, I can handle it. What huge character flaw do I possess that makes it impossible to share important information with me?"

She didn't stop the palm scratching.

"You're not the easiest person in the world to talk to, Calma."

"I suppose I'm not. Talking requires people to share the same space. Or are you saying it's difficult to be around me? Is that it? You can't even bear to be in the same room as me?"

She snapped her head up.

"Of course not. I'm not saying this is your fault. It's not. It's mine. But at the same time, you've got to admit you make judgments quickly, and they're not always nice or fair. I should have told you. But I wanted to find the right time. I'm sorry."

"Did you know he's Vanessa's father?"

"No. I just found out. He told me he had a daughter, but he never mentioned her name. It didn't come up."

"All right. Give me the sordid details. No, on second thought, just the bare bones. Where you met, how you met, where it's heading."

The Fridge pulled a crumpled packet of cigarettes from her bag and lit one. She sucked the smoke into her lungs hungrily.

"We met at the casino," she said finally.

"How romantic!"

"Please," she said. "You wanted to hear and I'll tell you. But I could do without the sarcasm."

I didn't say anything.

"There's another reason I didn't mention him to you," she continued. "Mike is a police officer. You know that. He told me he interviewed you after the holdup at Crazi-Cheep. Well, he was at the casino for work. Now, you mustn't say a word about this to anyone, Calma. You've got to promise me."

I gave a slight nod.

"The police are investigating the casino. Money has gone missing and they suspect at least one of the employees has been siphoning it off. Trouble is, they didn't know how and they didn't know who. Mike was undercover, observing what was going on. He'd been watching me. A suspect, I suppose. Anyway, it seems that after a while he knew I was in the clear. So he approached me, asked if I'd help with investigations, an inside line of inquiry. But I couldn't tell anyone. They were all under suspicion. I've been passing stuff to the police through him and apparently they're close to making arrests."

She got up, fetched an ashtray, and continued.

"He made me swear I wouldn't tell a soul until the investigation was wrapped up. I couldn't tell you about him. But then something else happened. I'd meet him regularly, in secret, to give information. Neither of us intended it to happen, but . . . well, we discovered . . . feelings. We were developing . . . a relationship. We were trying to be professional, but it got to the stage where we had to admit how we felt. That was two weeks ago. I suppose I could have said something to you then—not about the investigation, but that there was someone in my life. I'm sorry I didn't. I guess I thought it would be better to wait until the whole investigation was over before letting you know."

Not only was this the longest speech I had heard from the Fridge in years, but it was the longest silence I'd maintained in the same period of time. I didn't know where to start. Slapping her round the face was the obvious option, but I restrained myself.

"Tell me, Mum," I said. "This 'investigation'—does anyone else know about it? Apart from you and Sherlock, I mean."

"Of course not. Not at the casino. I told you—it's a delicate operation."

"So the only way you know a dastardly crime has been committed is because Inspector Morse told you?"

"I asked you to cut the sarcasm, Calma."

"Sorry. I just want to get this right. Instead of going to work—the best place, I'd imagine, to carry out your under-cover role—you'd throw a sickie to meet up with 007. He'd hand you a two-way radio receiver pen, give you a pair of shoes with laser-controlled missiles, and maybe wire your under-wear. Am I getting warm?"

That got the Fridge to her feet. She didn't look pleased.

"How dare you, Calma? How dare you be so rude? You re-sent me. Maybe you've got reason. But there's no excuse for cheap jibes at the expense of someone you don't even know."

"Oh, I know him, Mum. I know all about him."

"How?" demanded the Fridge. "How do you know about him?" It was a good question, so I ignored it.

"He's a slimeball, Mum. He's a disgusting chauvinist who undresses you with his eyes. I know that from my own experi-ence. But I also know he is abusive toward Vanessa. His own daughter."

"What?" The Fridge was shocked to her frosty core. She stopped in the middle of pulling out another cigarette and stared at me. The anger had been wiped from her face. Now there was incomprehension. "What do you mean?"

"You want me to define abuse?"

"How do you know? Has Vanessa told you this?"

It was my turn to be shifty.

"I just know, all right?"

"Has Vanessa told you?"

"I've seen the marks."

"Has she told you her father has abused her?"

I'll give her that. The Fridge would make a good cross-examination lawyer. I decided to go with withering scorn.

"Of course not. Do you really think she's going to go around talking about it? That's not the way it happens, Mum. It's something kept secret, even from your best friend. But just because the shame is too great to admit doesn't mean it isn't going on. I know, Mum. I know."

"And what evidence do you have?"

"More than you've got for the great casino heist!" I was struggling and I knew it. The phone rang but we ignored it. "Look, Mum. You know as well as I do that sometimes you don't have firm evidence—no smoking gun, no fingerprints or DNA samples—but you know inside what's the truth. Trust me on this. Please. The guy is poison. He's hurting Vanessa. I'm sure of it."

The Fridge lit another cigarette. Her hands were trembling as she took a drag, but when she spoke her voice was surprisingly strong and steady.

"Thanks, Calma, but I don't need a sermon on trust from someone who is ridiculing everything I'm saying. I'll tell you what, though. I won't undermine you. In fact, I'll acknowledge that it is valid to trust your instincts if you'll acknowledge mine. Sometimes, despite 'feelings,' the absence of evidence might indicate someone is innocent. What do you think?"

"Him or me, Mum. Do you trust him or me?"

"That's cheap and unfair. This has nothing to do with Mike. The question you are asking is do I trust your feelings or mine?"

I waved my hands around helplessly. I hate finding myself in an argument where I'm being outmaneuvered. It doesn't happen often.

"Okay, then," I said. "So which is it?"

She laughed and I almost hated her for it.

"You'll learn one thing in time, Calma," she said. "You *have* to trust yourself, because if you can't, then you might as well give up on everything."

"You're wrong about him."

"It's possible. But I can't accept it just because you say it."

"It'll end in tears."

The Fridge placed the cigarette on the edge of the ashtray. She seemed, suddenly, very tired.

"It normally does, Calma. It normally does."

The phone continued to ring in the background.

# Chapter 24

## Many miserable returns

The clock flicked over to midnight. I watched, fascinated, as it ticked off the minutes, relentlessly, remorselessly. Nothing could stop it. Even if I turned off the power, time would click by nonetheless, taking me step by step into the future. I stared at the glowing green digits, divided by a pulsing colon, and realized another year had turned over.

Seventeen.

There was no excitement in the word and I wondered why. Then a zero flickered and was destroyed by the appearance of a one. It felt like a countdown, my life flicking on and on while I lay on my side, powerless to prevent it.

*Happy birthday to you,*
*Happy birthday to you,*
*You look like a monkey*
*And you smell like one, too.*

All I could manage was a stupid rhyme. A silly chant from

primary school. No, I didn't feel excitement. I felt sad. Even as I watched another digit clocking up, I knew I was bathing in self-pity. The trouble was, it felt good. I clung to it like a birthday present.

Eventually I fell asleep. I don't know if I dreamed, but when I woke my head felt thick and woolly. The morning hadn't brought any answers. But it had brought an idea. Even as the Fridge bustled into my bedroom with a cooked breakfast, a card, and forced cheeriness, I turned the idea round and examined it from every possible angle. It didn't shine. It didn't glitter with hope. The more I looked at it, the duller it seemed. But it was the only idea I had.

The Fridge explained that she would hand over my present at the restaurant, a small Thai place on the riverfront. She had booked for four people, which came as a relief. I'd had this horrible feeling she'd been planning to unveil the slimeball over the beef massaman and tom yum goong. True, it would have given me the opportunity for a few choice words.

Waiter: *Can I interest you in the phat prik sod?*

Calma: *I doubt it. But bring him over anyway, will you?*

But on balance, I wasn't prepared to sit there all evening, head down, while Nessa's dad leered at us and inhaled rice noodles. I wouldn't have gone. Maybe the Fridge realized that and felt it was a confrontation best avoided. Whatever. I was to meet her there at seven. She would go straight to the restaurant from work. I'd tell Vanessa and Jason the arrangements.

I turned down the offer of a lift to school, claiming it was the perfect day for a bracing walk. It was a sign of the Fridge's distraction that she swallowed this. She drove off to destinations unknown and I walked in the opposite direction. And I don't mean the opposite direction from the Fridge. I mean the opposite direction from school. The time had come to put my idea to the test. I didn't hold out any great hopes, but fate had crapped in my back pocket—it was my only chance.

When I eventually arrived at school, about ten minutes before lunch, prospects had brightened. No guarantees, mind, but the whole thing had gone much better than I had dared hope. Now all I could do was wait.

There was no point trying to catch the last ten minutes of class, so I hung around the canteen, waiting for Vanessa. This took time, since she doesn't exactly race from class. Some species of amoebae could give her a head start in the hundred-yard dash and still ooze over the line first. But she finally turned up and I explained the evening's arrangements while she eroded yet another banana. There was barely time to get through this simple procedure before the warning bell rang for afternoon classes and we wandered over to the English block.

What a lesson! We discussed the poetry of Dylan Thomas, the roly-poly Welshman with the pickled liver of an alcoholic and the voice of an angel. If you never read another poem in your entire life, read "Fern Hill." It uses words in ways I'd never dreamed possible. It's language you can taste and feel. The ending brought a sharp swell of tears, an absurd mixture of happiness and pain. Quite literally, it took my breath away. I was still in my seat minutes after the lesson ended, my jaw scraping the desk, when Miss Moss came and sat opposite me. I had a study period next, so I wasn't in any hurry, and she must have had a free period too because there weren't any boys with sloping foreheads and non-opposable thumbs gibbering at the windows. I was hoping she wouldn't bring up my own attempts at poetry, which in comparison seemed pathetic, stale, and lifeless.

She didn't. She sat, head inclined, as if gathering her thoughts. I tried to blink back my absurd tears.

"Calma," she said finally, "I thought you'd want to know. I'm leaving the school at the end of term. I've been offered a job at another school and I can't afford to turn it down."

The tears I'd been trying to keep at bay returned with reinforcements. I shouldn't have been surprised that Miss Moss was leaving. I'd anticipated it. Nonetheless, the news hit me like a fist. I hung my head, and my eyes sought the poem, but the print was too blurry to read.

"I'm sorry," she continued. "If it's any consolation, the only reason I've even given any thought to staying on here is because of you. I'll miss you, Calma. It's not often you get a student who loves English like you do. And you have real talent. But I've got to make a living and there's no guarantee of permanent work here."

I lifted my head and brushed impatiently at the corner of one eye. It was ridiculous to spout like this.

"Why not?" I said.

She cupped her face in her hands, elbows fixed on my desk. I looked her in the eyes and there was sadness there.

"The only option here is another ten-week contract. Even then, assuming I get one, there's nothing to say I'll be teaching English. To be honest, the prospect of teaching IT or drama to a bunch of Year Nine boys full of testosterone doesn't appeal. *This* is what I love, Calma. Teaching English." She nodded toward the poetry book on my desk. "And I've been given a wonderful opportunity. Sanderson has offered me a full-time, permanent post. In English. I can't turn it down."

I closed the book slowly and reached for my bag. Never let it be said that Calma Harrison doesn't know the right way to behave, that she can't see the big picture. Although I felt like something had dropped beneath me, my voice was surprisingly strong and even.

"I'd be disappointed if you even thought about staying, Miss Moss," I said. "You are, by a long way, the best English teacher I've ever known. To stay here would be like asking Van Gogh to paint by numbers or Ian Thorpe to wear floaties. The only thing that surprises me is that you weren't snapped up long before this."

Miss Moss smiled and touched me gently on the arm.

"Calma, you're a remarkable student and a remarkable young lady. Promise to keep in touch. I want to help you in your studies, your poetry. We can't let that slip away."

I stood up and slung my bag over a shoulder. My smile wasn't even forced.

"Don't worry," I said. "You don't get rid of me that easily."

*Bloody oath*, I thought as I left the classroom. *No way*. I was ready for a change. Nearly five years at the school and it hadn't got better in all that time. Not really. The only thing that worried me was whether I could insist, when I enrolled at Sanderson next term, that they put me in Miss Moss's English class.

Jason sounded strange when I rang him after school to let him know the arrangements for my birthday bash. Even though I don't have a wealth of experience in matters of the heart, I understood the nature of the problem. And I couldn't blame him. When he wished me a happy birthday, it was with a brittle edge of insincerity, as if what he really wanted to say was, *Eat excrement and die, you bald loser.* I knew I would have to build bridges with Jason. When I considered it from his point of view, I realized I would have been frosty as well. So many incidents, so many dramatic episodes in our short relationship, and had I explained any of them? Not one. I hadn't even returned his calls after the flight from the Fridge's love nest. He deserved answers and I vowed I'd give them to him. I was lucky he didn't chuck me there and then. But he didn't. He told me he would pick me up at six-thirty and then we'd collect Nessa.

Maybe after the meal we'd have a chance to talk.

At least I had some time to think about it as I showered. I kneaded my scalp into a foamy lather, idly wondering how much money I was saving the Fridge on shampoo and conditioner. When it came time to towel off, I noticed my head was left with little speckles of red lint where the material had caught. I wiped off the condensation from the mirror and looked more closely. My hair was growing back. True, I was still bankrupt in the flowing locks department, but there was a dark stubble all over. My head was turning into Velcro. I brushed off the snagged fibers and went to work on my makeup.

I was ready by six and, if I say so myself, fairly resplendent. I'd gone for discreet glasses (I was tired of eyeballs that felt as though they'd been marinated in household bleach), black cargo pants, and a black cotton blouse. Chic, I thought. Plus, if my country needed me, I could be parachuted behind enemy lines to assassinate a tin-pot dictator without having to change. As the evening turned out, I'd have probably had more fun doing that.

Jason arrived right on time and I did my best to be upbeat and charming. He kissed me on the cheek (not a good sign— it was one of those air kisses Hollywood stars have perfected) and told me I'd get my present at the restaurant. I toyed with the idea of having a brief word then—you know, a quick apology and a promise that all would be revealed later on—but he was back in the car before I could open my mouth.

We drove to Nessa's in silence. The rush of air and the roar of the engine made conversation impossible and I didn't feel he was in the right mood for my mouth pressed intimately against his ear. We parked in Nessa's drive and I jumped out. Vanessa opened the door. I bobbed my head around her shoulder but couldn't see her mum. I didn't know if that was a good sign or not. Nessa looked stunning in a paisley caftan with matching headband. While I was slitting the throat of an imperial guard in the shadow-filled corner of a third-world palace, she could light candles for universal peace and sing "We Shall

Overcome." Jason, meanwhile, could do the stern-faced, un-communicative role of government spokesperson.

Nessa struggled under the weight of a gift-wrapped package of annoying dimensions—the sort that makes it impossible to guess what's in it. She also told me that I wasn't getting it until dinnertime. I know I should be more mature, but presents make me go all gooey with anticipation.

As we drove over the river, water sparkled and flashed with the reflections of lights strung along the banks. People moved lazily in front of shops, cafés, and restaurants. Night-market stalls were being assembled and a couple of early buskers had taken up positions, tuning their guitars and arranging their open cases expectantly. A few stars gleamed above the palm trees and the air was sweet with spices. It was peaceful.

**From:** Miss Moss <moss.aj@lotis.edu.au>
**To:** Calma Harrison <harrison.c@lotis.edu.au>
**Subject:** Villanelle

---

Calma,

It's time to try the villanelle form. This is a very rigid poetic structure and the basic rules are: sixteen or nineteen lines; iambic pentameter; four (or five) stanzas of three lines and a concluding four-line stanza; the first line of the poem is repeated as the final line of the second and fourth stanza; the third line of the poem is repeated as the final line of the third and (possibly) fifth stanza; the first and third lines come together as a final rhyming couplet; the rhyme scheme is *aba aba aba aba abaa.*

Couldn't be more straightforward!

Don't worry. It is a very difficult form and often used simply as an exercise in rhythm and rhyme. Very few villanelles are actually any good because the structure is so prescriptive. The magnificent exception to this is Dylan Thomas's *Do Not Go Gentle into That Good Night.* Read it and weep!

Good luck,
Miss Moss

## Villanelle for Jason

Don't think this silence speaks—that I don't care
For you, and draw dark shutters of the mind.
Look in my eyes and read the message there.

The spur is sharp, but not enough to dare
Those words my tongue just cannot bear to find.
Don't think this silence speaks—that I don't care.

I cannot tell you all, I cannot tear
Up stillness by its roots, but stumble, blind.
Look in my eyes and read the message there.

I think you sense a rift beyond repair,
And to our parting have become resigned—
Don't. Think! This silence speaks that I don't care?

That is absurd. Trust grows, in time (like hair!)
And bald resentments will be left behind.
Don't think this silence speaks, that I don't care—
Look in my eyes and read the message there.

# Chapter 25

## Thai died

The Fridge hadn't arrived when we got to the restaurant, but the waiter showed us to our reserved table. Jason still sported a mouth like a cat's bum, so I took charge of the drinks order. I went for the house chardonnay. Okay, I was still a year away from the legal drinking age, but it was my birthday, and anyway, the waiter's eyes were so transfixed on my chest he wouldn't have thought to ask for ID. Vanessa was in a good mood, because she ordered something like a tropical rainforest. I half expected David Attenborough to peep out over the rim of the glass, parting fronds and speaking in hushed tones. Jason had a beer.

All well and good. But conversation wasn't exactly zipping along. Nessa, as you know, wouldn't have been out of place in a religious order bound by a vow of silence. She blinked occasionally over the foliage of her drink, doing a remarkable impersonation of a potted plant. Jason's eyes slid all over the place but managed to avoid mine. We had the animation of three paving slabs. I went for a subtle icebreaker.

"Come on, you buggers," I said. "Give me presents."

But that didn't work. Jason and Nessa refused to hand anything over until the Fridge deigned to make an appearance. They didn't know her like I did. I just hoped they hadn't got me anything perishable. My cheery gambit spurned, I opted for humility. Or maybe it was simple begging.

"C'mon, guys," I said. "It's my birthday. I know I've been strange lately, but . . . well, it's my birthday." Lame, I admit, but the silence was getting to me. "Good cheer is customary. Animated conversation, the spontaneous carrying of the birthday girl in a chair around the restaurant to the lilt of amusing birthday songs. Frankly, at the moment, this could be the annual meeting of the local undertakers' association. Perhaps we could start with a smile and, if no one dies, see where that gets us?"

Jason finally looked at me. He had an I've-been-treated-in-a-very-shoddy-fashion-so-I've-the-right-to-behave-like-an-anal-sphincter air of grievance, but my words had clearly chipped at his resolve. I could see a flash of light soften his eyes and it wasn't just the reflection of candlelight. Once again, I felt a lurching in the pit of my stomach like the one I'd experienced when I first set eyes on him.

## Fact File

*Common name:* Jason Evans

*Scientific name: Hunkia britannica*

*Habitat:* Originally from England, the *Hunkia britannica* is a rare example of a successful foreign invader. It has flourished in the climate of Australia and is regarded by all observers as a particularly magnificent example of non-indigenous fauna. Can be enticed from its regular habitat into the arms of human beings by careful maneuvering and encouraging remarks about soccer.

*Mating habits:* Devoutly to be wished.

*Appearance:* Tall, rangy, and athletic in appearance, the *Hunkia britannica* is a splendid physical specimen. Beautiful skin tone, finely toned musculature, deep brown eyes liquid with sensitivity and eroticism, dribble, dribble, dribble.

*Toxicity:* Nontoxic. Pleasurable feelings of well-being can be achieved if rubbed against skin.

*Status:* Divine.

Jason opened his mouth—and then the Fridge materialized dramatically at his side.

She took off her jacket like it was an unaccustomed action.

Her fingers were shaking and her face was so lined it looked as if it had been slept in. There was a small tic near the corner of her right eye and her mouth was pulled down. She got rid of the jacket and didn't even glance in our direction. Jason was on his feet, showing manners more at home in the late nineteenth century. It was clear the Fridge didn't know who the hell he was. She even gave him the jacket, probably expecting him to exchange it for a wine list. Jason arranged it carefully on the back of her chair.

"Hello, Mrs. Harrison," he said. "It's good to see you again."

The Fridge blinked. I could see her summon her willpower in an attempt to occupy the time and space the rest of us filled. It was as if she was returning from some place far away.

"Jason," she said. "Yes. You too." Her voice was overly cheery, with little fault lines at the edges. In that moment I felt intensely sad. It was silly. I knew what had happened. It was written all over her. And it was what I had been praying for. Yet sudden tears stung my eyes.

The Fridge sat down and pulled her chair toward the table. She smiled, but it was nothing more than a series of muscle stretches.

"Hey, birthday girl," she said, finally making eye contact. "Sorry I'm late. I . . . I had to make a phone call. Have you ordered? Ah, drinks. Yes . . . Jason, be a love, will you, and attract the waiter's attention. How are you, Vanessa?"

But she didn't take her eyes from me.

The Fridge ordered a bourbon and Coke and didn't stop chattering. I took the opportunity to get another glass of wine.

I had a feeling I was going to need all the artificial courage I could find this evening. A large part of me wanted the silence back.

"Well, seventeen. Who would have thought it? It seems like yesterday . . . Oh, by the way, your present. I hope you like it."

She reached into her bag and pulled out an oblong package. She handed it across the table and it felt solid and heavy in my hands.

"I didn't know what to get you. It's so difficult. I mean, you've reached the age where I can't get you clothes. I have no idea what kind of music you like—it all seems foul-mouthed nowadays and chanted by large people with an unhealthy interest in drive-by shootings. That's if you can have a *healthy* interest in drive-by shootings. Anyway, if they haven't got a criminal record, they just record one. Hah! Calma, don't just sit there like a brick. Open your present!"

I wanted to get up and hug her. Instead I pulled away the wrapping. It was a book. A leather book, with gilt on the edges.

I could smell its age. I opened it to the flyleaf. *The Complete Works of Shakespeare,* dated 1821, with a foreword by the Reverend Bowdler. It was perfect.

"Oh, Mum," I said. For once, I was lost for words. I ran my hands over the leather binding and put it carefully on the table, well away from the pools of condensation puddling by the water carafe. Then I got up and the Fridge stood and we hugged. I squeezed hard, my arms around her waist, my head on her left shoulder. She smelled of Givenchy and defeat.

"Mum, I'm so sorry," I whispered. The words felt like something solid lodged in the back of my throat.

She increased the pressure of her arms around me before putting her hands on my shoulders and stepping back. Her smile was small and broken.

"Me too, sweetie," she said. "Me too."

ReWND™

Mrs. Aldrick was surprised to see me, which I suppose was understandable. She'd seen Vanessa off to school. She knew I should have been there too. Maybe, as we faced each other on the doorstep and I stared her straight in the eye, she knew why I had come. I suppose I'll never know.

At first she didn't want me to come in. She made excuses, but I was having none of it. She was the only solution. For Vanessa's and Mum's sake, I needed her to listen and I wasn't leaving until I'd given it my best shot.

We sat in the unnervingly spotless kitchen. She looked at me as if I was the manifestation of all her fears—a past that she hoped was dead and buried but which had quickened and returned to haunt her. As I talked, she ran her fingers over the polished surface of the table, her eyes darting around as if for aid.

I told her everything I suspected and, even as she tried to deny it, the doubts gnawing at me disappeared. Her words were nothing compared to the way the sinews in her arms moved, the slump of her shoulders, the relentless flickering of her eyes. It was all true.

When I got to the marks I'd seen on Vanessa's body, she inhaled sharply and her face twisted. I got the impression she'd hoped against hope that what had been in the past had remained there, that her daughter was safe. Wishful thinking. Maybe deep down Mrs. Aldrick knew, but it was a knowledge she was desperate to avoid. I forced her to face it.

I begged her to keep Vanessa at home from now on, to stand up to her ex-husband for her daughter's sake. I explained the research I had done on restraining orders and the process by which you could apply for one. It seemed bizarre—I was barely seventeen, yet I was advising someone over twice my age on issues that left my tongue coated with distaste. Neither of us wanted to have this conversation. Yet I floundered on, pushing words through the barrier of her silence. I told her about the Fridge, that there were two people she could protect if she summoned the courage. I gave her Mum's shift times for today. I'd got them by calling the casino. I couldn't force her to do anything. I didn't try. I just gave the information, sprinkled the seeds, hoped for germination.

When I left the house, she was sitting at the kitchen table, dragging her fingers over the surface, eyes fixed on the pattern of smudges she'd created. Mrs. Aldrick had made no promises. She had barely spoken. But I felt an irrational hope and it warmed me all the way to school.

FastF™

At least the Fridge's handing over of her present liberated Jason and Nessa from their smug self-discipline. Vanessa passed me her package, a lumpy and appallingly heavy object. I nearly pulled a muscle as I took it from her. For a moment, I thought she'd bought me a boulder. But it turned out to be a sandstone Buddha, intricately carved and full of tranquil flowing lines.

"Put it in your bedroom, Calma," said Vanessa. "In the corner where the chest of drawers is. It should counteract the strong yang energy in the room, as well as dissipating the shar chi, the killing breath, caused by the inauspicious juxtaposition of your wu xing."

"You couldn't run that by me again, could you?" I replied.

"Feng shui."

"That's a relief," I said. "I thought there was something wrong with you. It's lovely, Nessa. Thank you."

"And here's mine," said Jason. At least his present was small and didn't look like it might induce a hernia just opening it. I moved the Buddha to the edge of the table, where it threatened to tip the whole thing over, catapulting the water jug into the laps of diners over my shoulder. I ripped at the packaging on Jason's gift. I'm not the kind who patiently peels back sticky tape and methodically unfolds wrapping paper. I'm more the rampaging rend-and-shred-with-the-nails type, scattering paper like confetti.

It was a cell phone. A lovely, shiny cell phone—the kind that flips open. There was a small lens at the back. I'm not technically minded, but it looked like a phone with a still-image manipulator, video capture card, wireless Internet and espresso-making facility.

I was stoked.

Now I could do what everyone else did at school—develop

weak eyes by fiddling with the settings or installing ring tones of execrable taste.

"Thought it's something you could use," said Jason. "You can be a very difficult person to get hold of."

"It's brilliant. Thank you. I don't deserve it, Jason."

"Too right. You don't."

He didn't say it in a nasty way, though, and I knew we'd be all right. Later on, when there was just the two of us, I'd explain. I'd explain everything. And he'd kiss me and tell me he understood and that he thought I was a brilliant girlfriend and a wonderful friend and caring daughter, and we'd download ring tones until our fingers ached. I wanted to use it right away, but he explained I'd have to call the service provider to activate the SIM card.

"How can I do that?" I asked. "I don't have a working phone."

He took out his cell and gave it to me.

"There you go, Miss Impatient," he said. "Follow the directions on the card."

It took a while to work out how to turn his bloody phone on, but I managed to get through all the steps for activation. The service provider guy told me it would take a minute to do whatever he had to do, but basically I would be connected almost immediately.

"Course, you need to charge the phone up for about two hours before you can use it," Jason chipped in.

"What?"

"I'm pulling your plonker! I've already charged it. Calma, I think you're ready to join the world of electronic communication. Who you gonna call?"

I realized there wasn't anyone. The only people I cared about were sitting a foot away. Jason suggested I call him, but that was just too sad. Anyway, I had a better idea.

I punched in the number and there it was. My first call. Someone picked up after three rings.

"Hello?"

"Hello. This is table twelve. Any chance of someone taking our order?"

There was a puzzled pause, but it did the trick. A young man was over before I could flip my phone shut. We ordered and I took the opportunity to get another glass of wine. Despite the expression on the Fridge's face, a strange combination of happiness and misery, like she'd been violently sandbagged from behind in the middle of a wedding party, I was feeling fine. And it wasn't only because of the alcohol suffusing my bloodstream and buggering around with electrical impulses in my brain. It was good to be with these people.

Once we'd ordered, Jason showed me how to use the camera on the phone and I snapped away happily. I took pix of the three of them, the Fridge in the middle with her arms around Jason and Nessa. I took pix of my presents. I even got Jason to take one with his phone of my phone. I balanced it up against the Buddha so it appeared that the divine one was ordering a pizza. Boy, this wine was strong.

My father arrived halfway through the appetizers.

I was dipping the last of my fishcakes into a small puddle of sweet chili sauce when I became aware of someone standing next to the table. He ran a hand over his scalp and glanced nervously around. I swallowed the final morsel and took a sip of chardonnay. I was cool.

"Can I help you?" I said.

His eyes flitted everywhere and I saw more clearly than ever what a weak, contemptible creature he was.

"I'm going," he said. "Back to Sydney. Thought you'd want to know."

I brandished my new phone.

"Would you like me to call a taxi?" I said sweetly.

That shook him. He struggled to keep his temper and failed. Typically, what followed was bluster.

"You'll be sorry," he said, his voice rising in pitch. "And when I'm gone, it'll be too late for you to change your mind. There'll be no point crying to me then."

I raised my glass in a mock toast.

"Have a good trip," I said cheerfully.

He left then. The last I saw of him was a drooping figure slinking off into the darkness.

Vanessa's father arrived halfway through the main course. A shadow loomed over the table and I froze with the fork poised.

Nessa's dad didn't look as if he was about to add his personal best wishes to the celebration. Watery blue eyes washed coldly over us, before settling on the Fridge. Nessa nearly choked on her vegetable stir-fry.

"Dad!" she said, her voice thin and timid. "What are you doing here?"

He ignored her.

"Jean. A word. Now," he said.

It took a moment for the Fridge to recover her composure. She looked faintly sick and her brow was rumpled as if with a migraine. She placed her knife and fork slowly down onto her plate.

"Not now, Mike, please. This is my daughter's birthday meal. I'll call you later."

He grabbed her wrist.

"Not 'later,' Jean. Now. Outside."

Jason was on his feet immediately. Nessa's dad turned his head slowly and looked at him like he was something you'd find on the bottom of your shoe.

"Can I help you, sonny?" he said.

There was silence. I could feel tension knotting my muscles. The Fridge twisted her hand to break the grip. She kept her head lowered.

"I'm not going outside with you, Mike. I'm not going anywhere with you. It's finished. Don't you understand that?"

The expression on his face darkened. Rage writhed across his features. He slammed his fist down on the table and a jug fell over. A stream of water flowed across the tablecloth and onto the floor. The only noise in the whole restaurant was the sound of dripping. He bent his head towards the Fridge.

"No one does this to me. Do you hear me? No one." His

voice was low and tight with malice. "I decide when things are over. *I* decide. And you are going to regret this. Trust me. You are going to seriously regret this."

"Dad, please . . ."

He jabbed a finger towards Vanessa and she cringed back in her chair.

"And as for you . . . ," he said. "You are going to wish you were never born."

"It's too late for that, Mike," said the Fridge. "She must already feel like that, thanks to you. But it's finished. You are never going to hurt any of us again."

It was like she had slapped his face. He took a step back and then the storm he carried within broke. His voice crashed over us, like thunder.

"You bitch!" he screamed. He clenched his fist and drew it back. At that moment I wasn't aware of doing anything, but I stood and my hand gripped something. In the second before his fist would have slammed into my mother's face, I brought forth lightning to match his thunder. The flash froze him. I held my phone up. The image was small but clear. You could see the arm raised and poised to strike, his features snarled into a grimace of dark joy. And there, cowering under the fist, a tired, frail and scared woman. I pointed the phone at him like it was a crucifix and he was the devil. He even stepped back a pace or two.

"I'm calling the police," I said. "You're through, Collins. We have witnesses"—I pointed around the restaurant—"and we have photographic evidence." I dialed the number. "You have a couple of minutes to run for your miserable life. Enjoy those minutes, because I promise you'll pay for your crimes. Calma Harrison will never rest until you pay."

He glanced nervously over his shoulder, as if realizing what he'd done. He didn't look so menacing now. As I talked to the police, he dashed to the front door, changed his mind and ran towards the restaurant's toilets. He was going for a back door, but it wouldn't do him any good. I had meant every word.

We sat at the table and waited for the police. The customers around us had started talking again. Shock was starting to bite. I kept my head down and tried to suppress the tears threatening to overflow. I felt a hand on my arm.

"Thanks, Calma," said Vanessa. "I feel safe now, safe for the first time in years. And it's all because of you."

I smiled and glanced over at the Fridge. She was smiling as well.

"I was a fool," she said. "I couldn't see it. I probably didn't want to see it. Thank God you were watching over me, Calma."

I couldn't say anything. My emotions were too tightly wound. Jason looked at me and there was admiration in his eyes. Admiration and . . . something more.

We held hands, the four of us, and waited for the police to come. A siren droned in the distance. It was getting closer. I felt at peace.

**Manuscript ends**
**Manuscript starts again . . .**

I remember Dad reading me a bedtime story, *Little Red Riding Hood*, when I was four or five. I hated that story. I didn't want Granny to be eaten. I didn't want the wolf to die. The best ending, it seemed to me, was for them to sort themselves out and become friends. Maybe the wolf could enroll in an anger management program, Granny could get hormone replacement therapy, Little Red Riding Hood could grasp the basics of stranger-danger and they'd live out their lives happily, going on picnics and playing croquet. Each time Dad read me the story, I'd hope for a different ending. But it never happened. The story had its own inflexible pattern. Maybe that's where it started—this disappointment when nothing turns out as you expect.

I tried, but it didn't work. You can't mess around with story. You can't mess around with life. I've learned so much recently. And one of the things I've learned is this: there is a difference between an unreliable narrator and a narrator who turns her back on the truth. You can like the first, but the second is contemptible. I can't expect you to like me. No. I can't expect that. But I can't bear your contempt.

So. I need to tell you what really happened, and to do that, we must revisit the restaurant. Even—especially—if the visit is painful for the narrator.

ReWND™

Once we'd ordered, Jason showed me how to use the camera on the phone and I snapped away happily. I took pix of the three of them, the Fridge in the middle with her arms around

Jason and Nessa. I took pix of my presents. I even got Jason to take one with his phone of my phone. I balanced it up against the Buddha so it appeared that the divine one was ordering a pizza. Boy, this wine was strong.

Halfway through the appetizers, a waiter tapped me on the shoulder.

"I'm sorry to interrupt your meal, madam, but there is a gentleman asking to speak to you. In the takeaway area." He pointed towards a glass door next to the bar. My expression must have been puzzled, because he added hastily, "He apologizes, but assures it won't take a moment."

I raised my eyebrows, but no one offered any advice, though I noticed the Fridge kept her head over her plate. I followed the waiter into a small area with a counter and a few chairs against the wall. There was a large takeout menu above the counter, next to a television mounted on a bracket. A newscaster was talking earnestly, but I didn't pay attention. The waiter gestured towards a man standing by the outer door and then ducked back into the restaurant.

My father.

I noticed, on the periphery of my vision, a woman sitting on a chair, flicking through a magazine while she waited for her food. I kept my eyes fixed on my father. Maybe it was the wine. Maybe I resented the intrusion into an intimate occasion. Whatever. His face irritated me. I folded my arms and glanced pointedly at my watch.

"Hello, Calma," he said.

"This is a private function," I replied. "If you've got something to say, be quick. I need to get back to my guests."

He shifted nervously on his feet and placed the tips of his fingers together.

"I'm sorry," he said. "Your mum told me you'd be here. And I wouldn't have come but . . ." He waved his hands vaguely. "I've run out of time. We're leaving tonight. Back to Sydney, on the midnight flight."

I said nothing. *We?*

"We never got the chance to talk," he continued. "Maybe your mum'll tell you what I wanted to say. If nothing else, I want you to know I'm sorry for the pain I've caused."

I snorted. Words are so cheap.

He made a movement towards me, the stirring of an embrace choked before it found life. For a brief moment, he stood there, arms stretched tentatively, before he dropped them to his sides.

"Goodbye, Calma."

The woman stood and threw the magazine on a littered coffee table. She moved to my dad's side and put an arm around his waist. It was so unexpected I felt paralyzed, even as I recognized her. The woman from Crazi-Cheep. The woman I had overcharged. The woman with the laugh. Kindness was still printed on her face, but overlaid with a patina of sadness. She looked into my dad's face, smiled and brushed something from his cheek. My stomach lurched at the pure affection in the gesture. She turned her eyes to me.

"It's been lovely meeting you, Calma. Thanks again for the laughs. I had hoped we . . . well, maybe under different circumstances . . ." She smiled, and it was warm, genuine. I didn't hear the door open behind me. I didn't know the Fridge was there until she moved past and into my line of vision. She hugged my father and then the woman. They kissed cheeks.

"Goodbye, Bob. Sally. Great to see you. Have a good flight and stay in touch."

"Thanks, Jean. Look after yourself. And Calma, of course. We'll call."

"Do that."

I couldn't move. It was as if my muscles had locked while my brain grappled with things I couldn't understand. They moved towards the door and I did nothing to stop them. The woman had her hand on the doorknob when my father turned. He was smiling slightly.

"Just thought I'd tell you. Love the hairdo. Very chic. Very New Age."

My reply was out before I knew it. I noted, distantly, that my voice was low and brittle.

"Shave for a Cure. The Leukemia Foundation."

"Yeah, I know." His smile widened. "And I appreciate it."

And then they were gone, swallowed by darkness. Everything was still, apart from the drone of the TV. The Fridge put an arm around my shoulder. I stared at the door.

"Who was she?" I said.

"Sally Harrison. Your dad's wife. Your step-mum."

"She's the barmaid?" I didn't get it. The Fridge sighed and sat me down in a worn chair. She took the seat next to me.

"Calma," she said. Her voice was quiet, soothing. "There was no barmaid."

"But you told me . . ."

"No. I never said she was a barmaid. She was the service manager in a hotel here. I told you that. Many times. But you wouldn't listen. You had an image in your head and nothing would budge it. Not even the truth."

I shook my head. This was seriously weird.

"He didn't contact me. He never tried to tell me . . ."

The Fridge took my hands in hers.

"Calma, he sent you letters. You ripped them up. He phoned. You refused to take the calls. Eventually he gave up. But he tried. He tried for years. The sad truth is, you didn't."

I stood up, and paced. What the Fridge was saying didn't gel with my memories. I was confused. I stopped under the TV and faced her. Something strange rose from the turmoil of my thoughts.

"He didn't come back for a reconciliation," I said.

The Fridge laughed.

"He's happily married, Calma. I'm happy that he's happy. And, no, he never wanted that sort of reconciliation. Bob and I were reconciled long ago. All he wanted was to talk to you."

"I was wrong." It was a disturbing conclusion. I had difficulty even uttering the words. The Fridge smiled.

"You were wrong."

There were too many things churning in my mind. I sat down again, head in hands, and dimly heard Jason come in. He talked to the Fridge, asked if I was okay, and the Fridge told him to give us a couple more minutes. The door closed. The wine didn't help. I was trying to pin things down, get them arranged neatly in my mind, but the alcohol swirled them away. At least I'd helped the Fridge and Nessa. That was a comfort and I clung to it like a lifeline. We didn't have to worry about Mike Collins. Inspector Mike Collins.

Wait a moment. I hadn't thought that. The words continued and they were out there somewhere. In the room.

"Inspector Mike Collins was unavailable for comment, but it is understood he led the investigation, codename Royal Flush, which resulted in the arrest earlier today of four senior employees at the city casino. Charges of fraud are expected to be laid and sources at the casino indicate the alleged scam involved hundreds of thousands of dollars. And now in sports . . ."

The television presenter gave a smile and the screen changed. I turned, slowly, robotically, towards the Fridge. She gazed at the floor and scratched her nose.

"Ah, yes," she said. "You were wrong about that, too."

We didn't finish the meal. We didn't even get through our main course. To be honest, I don't remember much. The Fridge and I went back in, but I didn't have an appetite. Jason asked me if I was all right and I shouted at him. Told him to mind his own business. Something horrible, anyway. He left. Pushed his chair back and stormed out. I didn't stop him. Nessa was biting her nails. She looked terrified. No one objected when the Fridge suggested we go. She paid the bill and we left. I sat in the back of the car. The Fridge dropped Vanessa off at home and we watched as her mum let her in. I said nothing the entire trip. Too much mental chaos.

It's strange. Sometimes, a little thing can stick in your mind, demanding attention, even if you are overwhelmed with other, more important, thoughts. It was like a mental splinter. Whenever my mind brushed it, it pricked. We were pulling into our driveway.

"What did Dad mean by appreciating it? My shave-for-leukemia?"

The Fridge turned off the engine and sighed. I watched the back of her head. The engine ticked as it cooled.

"We need to talk," she said.

"What did he mean?"

"He's dying, Calma. That's what he came to tell you."

**From:** Miss Moss <moss.aj@lotis.edu.au>
**To:** Calma Harrison <harrison.c@lotis.edu.au>
**Subject:** Improvisation

---

Calma,

Do you remember the saxophone? I sometimes bring it to class to make a point about writing. Too many people think they *know* words, simply because they use them in everyday situations. They never *learn* what language can and cannot do. My analogy is that it is impossible to create unique, meaningful music from a saxophone, *unless you know the rules of music* first and have practiced extensively. Only then can you improvise, find your own voice, maybe by breaking those rules.

You have put time into your scales, Calma. Now compose your own music, in your own way.

Play for me.
Miss Moss

## The blank page

The blank page lies before me, still:
White space that I can fill
With worlds and lives within them.
I aim to share this God-like stratagem,
To unfold all from nothingness to being
And, in black ink, reflect what I am seeing.
Yet words are fires against my dark self-doubt,
I write to flush the shifting shadows out.

And if I stop to think, it seems
Tomorrows are a set of different pages
On which to write. The future teems
With what might be. Though story's torrent rages,
Sweeps characters from was to will be,
I know I have the mind and heart
To plot my course and follow where it leads me.
I start where all the worthwhile journeys start:
White space that I can fill—
The blank page lies before me still.

# Chapter 26

## Fallout

"Why didn't you say anything?"

We sat in the kitchen. A box with a birthday cake in it was on the table between us. The restaurant had kept it in the kitchen, waiting for the signal from the Fridge to bring it in, ablaze with seventeen candles. The signal never came.

"I couldn't, Calma."

"Why not?"

"Your father wanted to tell you himself. He said he had messed up the last time and it was his responsibility to repair some of the damage. I couldn't take that away from him."

I was drinking water to wash away the alcohol and the confusion. It wasn't working. There were so many questions and I didn't know where to start. So I just let them pop out by themselves.

"What about Vanessa? Those cuts and scratches. Her dad did them. Her mum more or less told me."

Mum topped up her wine glass. She'd opened a bottle as soon as we got in. There wasn't much left.

"I talked to Vanessa's mother," she said, running a finger around the rim of the glass. "She came to see me at the end of my shift. That's partly why I was late for the restaurant. She was almost hysterical. Poured out all this stuff about you coming round, making outrageous accusations."

"But she didn't argue much. And her body language told me all I needed to know." I was working up some indignation. I wasn't completely wrong. I couldn't be.

The Fridge looked so tired. She tipped her glass and contemplated the liquid swishing around.

"I'm sure her silence spoke volumes. Trouble is, you weren't listening. She was stunned, Calma. Look at it from her point of view. She opens the door and there's her daughter's best friend, who casually informs her that she—the wife—has been physically and emotionally abused by her ex-husband. Worse, that he is now abusing her daughter. She knows it's nonsense, but she doesn't know how to react. She just wants you out of the house. Of course she kept quiet. It was the quickest way to get rid of you."

"No," I said. "That can't be right. What about the cuts and scratches? I *saw* them, Mum. They didn't happen by themselves and they didn't happen by accident. Someone did that to her."

The Fridge finished what was in her glass and went to pour another. She examined the contents of the bottle and thought better of it.

"Yes," she said. "You're right. Someone did. That was another reason I was late. I talked to Mike. He wasn't keen to discuss it, but I pushed him. There's a long history, Calma. It's been happening for years. Vanessa does it herself. She's a self-harmer."

We talked for hours. I brought up the episode in the police station, when Nessa's dad had undressed me with his eyes. Slimeball.

"No," said the Fridge.

He *was* staring at me. He recognized my name. There aren't many Calma Harrisons, after all. He was curious. In fact, he volunteered to interview me, even though robbery wasn't his area. He was in the fraud section. I was distraught. I was mistaken. Could I have been mistaken? I thought back. I hadn't looked directly at him, just felt his eyes on me. It was possible.

The more we talked, the more things came into focus. The self-harming had started just after Vanessa's parents split. She cut herself on the arms and wrists. She'd take time off from school and then return covered with bandages. Accident-prone. That's how it was explained. She saw counselors. Her mum became increasingly nervous, worried about her daughter. She was on the verge of a breakdown. This must have made Vanessa feel guilty. She probably felt responsible for her mother's state, and trips to her father's house were increasingly a way out of a disturbing environment. But she must also have felt guilty about that, seeing it as a betrayal of her mother. No one knew the self-harming had started again. Not until I brought it up. Vanessa kept it hidden. It was classic behavior.

I arranged all the pieces in my head and saw they fitted. I cried. I cried for my father, for the pain I had caused Vanessa's mum, for the damage I had done to the Fridge. Most of all I cried for Vanessa. She deserved so much help and support. I'd given her nothing. What had she said, that day at school? "It's not all about you, Calma." But that was the way I had thought and behaved, even if it wasn't conscious. And yes, at the back of my mind there was a small reserve of tears for myself. Calma bloody big-shot Harrison.

Mum rocked me as I cried myself into exhaustion. She didn't say much, just let me vent some of the self-loathing. Towards the end, before I slumped into bed, she said one thing.

"Calma, it's okay to be wrong. It's okay. But it's what happens next that's important. You have a friend in pain. In trouble. How are you going to help her? Not by thinking you're worthless. By being strong. She needs you. Are you going to let her down?"

I slept a deep, dreamless sleep.

The morning brought a text message on my new phone. It was from Jason, dumping me. My first text message. I couldn't blame him. I deserved nothing less. I sat at the kitchen table and considered my options. And the more I thought, the better I felt. It was so strange. The day ahead was a blank page and I could write on it whatever I wanted. I just needed to be a more reliable narrator. I planned out the immediate future, like notes for a novel.

I would make the Fridge breakfast in bed. Later, I'd go to the bank and withdraw the forty-eight dollars sitting in my savings account. It wasn't much, but the Leukemia Foundation wouldn't turn it down. Then I'd go to Crazi-Cheep, to see if Candy could roster me on for more shifts. A trip to Sydney wasn't going to be cheap and I would have to budget for it. If I had time, I'd go over to Sanderson and pick up some enrollment forms.

I was also going to find Jason. It was time I enlightened him. First—you don't dump someone by text message. Second— you don't dump Calma Harrison. Even when she deserves it.

But between breakfast and the bank, I was going round to Nessa's house. I wasn't going to say anything about her injuries. I might be dumb in many ways, but I'm not *that* dumb. We would talk. I'd make her laugh. More than anything else, I'd listen. I'd build up her trust again slowly. I would be there for her and we'd get through this together. It was time for me to be a proper friend.

As I turned the Fridge's toast into carbon, it struck me that I might have made a mess of everything, but I was going to come out of this better, stronger and wiser.

I don't know. What do you think?

ReCRD™

## Acknowledgments

Top of all my lists: Nita, wife, friend, reader, critic, and greatest supporter. My children Lauren and Brendan read and liked the manuscript. Thanks to them for keeping me on track, particularly when I strayed from the strange, disturbing, and exciting world of teenage life. My daughters Kris and Kari lent support from an enforced distance. Their belief was, and is, very important to me. All my family, friends, colleagues, and students: I have been overwhelmed by your generosity, interest, and encouragement. Thanks also to Jodie Webster and Erica Wagner, of Allen & Unwin, Australia, for their enthusiasm and expertise and to Nancy Siscoe, of Knopf, USA, for her unwavering support and sensitive editing.

Barry Jonsberg was born in Liverpool, England, and now lives and works in Darwin, Australia. As a student, he was so desperate to avoid work that he stowed away in a university department for years, eventually emerging into the real world, blinking and pale, with two degrees in English literature.

His first book, *The Crimes and Punishments of Miss Payne*, was short-listed for the Children's Book Council Book of the Year Awards in Australia.

Barry is a supporter of Liverpool FC and, after the 2005 Champions League final, believes firmly in miracles. He also enjoys watching cricket and is still on a high after England's historic Ashes victory over Australia in 2005.